HOME TO TSUGARU

OSAMU DAZAI

Translated by
SHELLEY MARSHALL

Copyright © 2022 by Shelley Marshall

ISBN 978-1-7349644-5-5

Second edition

All rights reserved.

No part of this book may be reproduced in any form or by any electronic or mechanical means, including information storage and retrieval systems, without written permission from the copyright holder, except for the use of brief quotations in a book review.

www.jpopbooks.com

 Created with Vellum

CONTENTS

Introduction   v

1. The Pilgrimage   1
2. Kanita   8
3. Sotogahama   32
4. The Tsugaru Plain   69
5. The West Coast   105

Credits   141
About the Author   143

INTRODUCTION

The Snows of Tsugaru
Powdered snow
Grainy snow
Cottony snow
Wet snow
Packed snow
Crystalline snow
Icy snow

(from *The Eastern Ou Almanac*)

For the first time in my life, I spent three weeks one spring touring the Tsugaru Peninsula at the northern end of Honshu. It was the most important event of my thirty plus years of life. I was born and raised my first twenty years in Tsugaru. I was only familiar with the towns of Kanagi, Goshogawara, Aomori, Hirosaki, Asamushi, and Owani, and knew next to nothing about the other towns and villages.

I was born in the town of Kanagi. It is located almost

Introduction

in the center of the Tsugaru Plain and has a population of five or six thousand. This town boasts of no special features but puts on airs as if it were a city. On the good side, it is plain and simple like water. On the bad side, the town is shallow and conceited. A little over seven miles to the south along the Iwaki River lies Goshogawara. As the distribution center of local products, its population surpasses ten thousand. With the exception of the two cities of Aomori and Hirosaki, no other towns in the area have a population over ten thousand. On the good side, those towns are bustling. On the bad side, they are noisy. They lack the smells of farming towns, but the dreadful loneliness, a characteristic of cities, is already creeping into these small towns. I admit the comparison may be a bit exaggerated, but Kanagi could be likened to the scenic Koishikawa in Tokyo and Goshogawara to the entertainment district of Asakusa.

My aunt lives in Goshogawara. As a child, I was more attached to this aunt than to my birth mother. In fact, I often stayed at my aunt's home. Until my middle school days, you could say I was ignorant about any town in Tsugaru other than Goshogawara and Kanagi. When I traveled to Aomori to take the entrance exam for middle school, the trip lasted a mere three or four hours but felt like an expedition to me. I chronicled the drama of my excitement at that time in a novel. That depiction was not necessarily true and filled with fictional buffoonery, but, for the most part, my feelings were as written.

> My lonely chic known only to me grew richer in design year by year. When I graduated from the village grammar school, I rode in a swaying horse-drawn carriage board a train to the small city of the prefectural capital in order to take the middle school entrance exam.

Introduction

My boys' clothes at that time were eccentric. My white flannel shirt was, by far, the most pleasing article to me. Of course, I wore it. The large collar attached to this shirt resembled the wings of a butterfly. The shirt collar stuck out far enough to cover the collar of my kimono in the way the collar of an open-neck summer shirt covers the collar of a suit jacket. It may have looked like a bib. But the youthful me was pathetically nervous and my custom was to think I favored a young nobleman.

I wore short *hakama* trousers made from a white-striped Kurume-kasuri fabric, long socks, and shiny black, high-laced shoes. I also wore a cloak. My father was already dead, and my mother was sick. As a result, this youth was cocooned in the compassion of my older brother's kind wife. The youth took advantage of this sister-in-law and forced his shirt collar to be larger. She smiled but was actually angry. The youth's grief nearly brought him to tears because no one understood his sense of beauty.

"Chic. Elegance." The aesthetics of the youth were exhausted. No, every living thing, the entire purpose of life was exhausted. I didn't button my cloak on purpose and wore it so that it slid off my narrow shoulders. I believed that was stylish. Where did I learn that? I had no model to follow and may have naturally developed this instinct for style.

The reason I presented my tasteful appearance for once in my life was my debut at a real city for the first time in my life. The moment I arrived in this small city on the northern edge of Honshu in a state of overexcitement, the drastic change left my young self speechless. I taught myself to speak the Tokyo dialect from boys' magazines. But when I went to the inn and heard the maids speak, they spoke in the Tsugaru dialect, exactly

Introduction

as they did in my hometown. The experience was a little anticlimactic. Twenty miles separated the town where I was born and that small city.

This small coastal city was Aomori. Here are some facts you may not know. As the premier seaport in Tsugaru, the Sotogahama magistrate began administration of this port in the first year of the Kan'ei era (1624), roughly three hundred and twenty years ago. In those days, one thousand houses already existed. The most successful ports were located in Sotogahama. Departing boats traveled to places like Omi, Echizen, Echigo, Kaga, Noto, and Wakasa, and its prosperity steadily grew. Aomori Prefecture was established by the order abolishing feudal domains and creating prefectures in Meiji year 4 (1871). The city of Aomori became the prefectural capital, now protects the northern gate to Honshu, and has a railway ferry service to Hakodate in Hokkaido.

Today, Aomori boasts more than twenty thousand households and a population exceeding one hundred thousand. Probably, no traveler finds this town friendly. The houses are unavoidably shabby because of frequent fires. The traveler hasn't the slightest clue about the location of the city center. Bizarrely sooty, expressionless houses line the streets and do not welcome the traveler who, feeling uneasy, dashes through town. However, I lived in Aomori for four years. I am writing about those pivotal years of my life in what will become a novel about my early years to be titled *Omoide* (Memories).

> My grades weren't good, but that spring, I passed the entrance exam to middle school. I dressed in new hakama trousers, black socks, and lace-up shoes. I replaced the blanket I had been using with a cloak styl-

Introduction

ishly left unbuttoned and open in front to travel to the small city on the sea. I took off my traveling clothes at a dry goods shop in town as a guest of distant relatives. At that shop with the old *noren* curtain falling off at the entrance, they took good care of me.

By nature, I easily become enthusiastic about anything. After I started school, I'd put on my school cap and hakama trousers to go to the public bath. When I saw my reflection in the window glass along the way, I smiled and gave myself a slight bow.

However, school wasn't the least bit interesting. The school campus was at the edge of town, and the buildings were painted white. Right behind the school was a flat park facing the strait. I could hear the sounds of the waves and the rustling pine trees during class. The halls were wide, and the classroom ceilings were high. All of that made me feel good, but the teachers persecuted me.

Beginning the day of the school entrance ceremony, I was belted by some phys ed teacher. He said I was a smart-aleck. This teacher was in charge of my oral exam when I took the entrance exam. He was kind to me and said I probably hadn't been able to study well because my father had died. I only hung my head. My heart hurt because he was the lone compassionate teacher. Later, I was smacked by various teachers. They'd punish me for a variety of reasons, among them were grinning and yawning. I was told the teachers concluded in the staff room that I yawned too much during class. I found it strange they discussed such nonsense in the staff room.

One day, another student who came from the same town called me over to the shadows of the sand dunes on campus. He warned me that my attitude came off as cocky and would result without fail in beatings. I was astonished. After classes were dismissed that day, I rushed home along the shore and sighed as I walked while waves licked the soles of my shoes. As I wiped the sweat off my forehead with the sleeve of my Western-style uniform, a surprisingly large gray sail passed unsteadily before my eyes.

This middle school is on the eastern end of Aomori today, unchanged from the past. That flat park is Gappo Park. It was close enough to the middle school to be considered its backyard. Except during winter blizzards, I cut through this park on the way to and from school and walked along the beach. This backstreet was used by few students and energized me. Mornings in the early summer were the best. The dry goods shop where I stayed was owned by the Toyoda family of Tera-machi and had a long-established, preeminent store in Aomori for close to twenty generations. The father died a few years ago. I was more precious to this man than his own children. I'll never forget that. I visited Aomori two or three times over the past few years, visited his grave each time, and always stayed with the Toyoda family.

One spring morning when I was a third-year student, on the way to school, I felt lightheaded for a short time and grabbed onto the cylindrical handrail stained red. A river wide like the Sumida River slowly flowed under the bridge. I never had the experience of feeling dizzy in the past. I felt I was being watched from behind and struck certain poses for some time. To each of my actions, he was bewildered and stared at his hands or watched while scratching the back of his ear but soon concocted an explanation. He was not convinced my actions were spontaneous or instinctive. After my senses returned on the bridge, I was unsettled by loneliness. When I had those feelings, I thought about my past and my future. Stumbling over the bridge, I remembered various events and dreamed. In the end, I sighed and thought, Maybe, I'll be a great man.

...

I had intimidating thoughts like, You must surpass the masses, but, in fact, I studied. After entering my third year, I was always at the top of my class. It was hard to be first in class without being called a grade grubber. I did not accept this ridicule and learned techniques to tame my classmates. Even the captain of the judo team, nicknamed Octopus, obeyed me. A large pot for wastepaper stood in the corner of the classroom. Occasionally, if I pointed to it and said, "Octopus, can you get in the pot?" Octopus stuck his head inside and laughed. His laughter echoed to produce bizarre sounds. The good-looking boys in class hung around me, too.

I stuck spots of adhesive plaster cut into the shapes of triangles, hexagons, and flowers on the pimples on my face, but nobody laughed. These pimples plagued me. Their number kept growing. When I opened my eyes each morning, I checked the state of my face by patting with the palm of my hand. I bought different medicines and dabbed them on my face, but they had no effect. When I went to buy medicine at the drugstore, I wrote the name of the medicine on a slip of paper and pretended I was asking if they sold that medicine for someone else. I thought pimples were a sign of sexual desire and was so ashamed everything before my eyes went black. I even thought about dying. The bad reputation of my face reached a peak among my family. My oldest sister who lived in another house warned no woman would become my bride. I diligently applied the medicines.

Introduction

My younger brother worried about my pimples, too, and often went to buy the medicine in my place. This brother and I hadn't gotten along since we were small. When he took the entrance exam for middle school, I hoped he would fail. But being far from home, I gradually discovered his nice disposition. As my brother got older, he became bashful and quiet. Once in a while, he and I published short literary works in our fanzine, but they were all timid compositions. Unlike me, he constantly fretted over his bad grades. And my sympathy only put him in a bad mood. He was annoyed by a growth the shape of Mt. Fuji swelling on his face into a part of a woman's physique. He was convinced he wasn't smart because his forehead was narrow. I forgave this brother anything and everything. In those days, I either hid everything from people or confessed everything to them. That brother and I confided everything to each other.

One moonless night at the beginning of fall, we went out to the pier of the harbor and commented on a fluttering red thread in the breeze blowing across the strait toward us. A Japanese language teacher at school once told this story in class. An invisible red thread was tied to the little toe of your right foot. The string smoothly stretched with one end tied to the same toe of a girl. No matter how far the two of us were separated, the thread would never break. No matter how close we were, even if we met on the street, that thread would never become entangled. This determined the girl who would become your bride. When I first heard this story, I got very excited and immediately told my brother when I returned home. That night, we talked as we listened to the sounds of waves and the calls of seagulls. When I asked my brother what is your wife doing now, after

Introduction

shaking the handrail along the pier a few times with both hands, he awkwardly said, "Walking in the garden." I thought the young woman wearing large garden *geta* clogs, holding a fan, and gazing at the primrose seemed perfect for my little brother. It was my turn, but looking off at the black sea, I only said, "Her *obi* sash is red." A ferryboat crossing the strait floated out unsteadily from the horizon and looked like a huge inn with its many rooms lit by yellow lights.

Two or three years later, my little brother died. At that time, we enjoyed going to the pier. On snowy nights in the winter, we carried umbrellas and went to the pier. In the sea of a deep harbor, the silent falling snow was spectacular. Lately, Aomori Port has become congested with ships. This pier is buried under ships and no longer a scenic location. Tsutsumi River, a wide river like the Sumida River, flowed on the eastern side of Aomori and into Aomori Bay. The river flowed slowly like a reverse flow at a spot right before pouring into the sea. I gazed absent-mindedly at that sluggish flow. If I were a pretentious man, I'd liken my youth to that point immediately before the river flowed into the sea. Those four years in Aomori were times I found hard to forget. For the most part, those were my memories of Aomori. Another unforgettable place is the seaside Asamushi Hot Springs, nearly seven miles east of Aomori. The following paragraph appears in *Memories*:

> Autumn came, and I left the city with my brother to go by train to the hot springs on the coast about thirty minutes away. After my mother fell ill, my youngest sister rented a house there to take the hot-spring cure. I stayed there the whole time and continued to study for my entrance exam. My troublesome reputation of being a

prodigy required me to display it from my fourth year in middle school until entering high school. During that time, I came to hate school. It was horrible, but as a person being pursued by something, I studied with single-minded determination. I took the train from there to school. Every Sunday, my friends came to pass the time. I always had a picnic with them. On flat rocks at the shore, we enjoyed meat stew and drank wine. My brother had a nice voice and knew many new songs. He taught us these songs, and we all sang together. We wore ourselves out fooling around and fell asleep on the rocks. When we woke up, the tide had come in. The rock, which should have been part of the shore, was an island. We felt as though we had not awakened from our dreams.

In the end, my joke is my youth was poured into the sea. The sea around Asamushi was cool and clear and not too bad. However, the inn could not be said to be good. The charm of a desolate fishing village in Tohoku was to be expected and not a flaw. Was I just a little arrogant like the frog in a well who knew nothing about the big ocean and was confused? I am bold and scoff at the hot springs in my hometown but am not bothered by the anxiety I felt when in the countryside far away. I haven't stayed at any hot springs in this area recently. Fortunately, the costs of staying at the inns have not become exorbitant. Clearly, I'm saying too much, but I haven't stayed here recently and gazed through the train window at the houses of the hot spring towns. These are only the words of the shallow intuition of a poor artist and have no foundation. However, I don't want to force my intuition on the reader. Rather, the reader may prefer not to believe my intuition. I believe Asamushi is starting over as a humble town for convalescence. For some time, the passionate, stylish crowd of Aomori City was electrified by this chilly hot springs area and became the proprietresses of inns to become like those in Atami and Yugawara. A fleeting suspicion crossed my mind that I may be intoxicated by an unwise illusion from my thatched cottage. The story tells of a warped, poor man of letters on a journey who never leaves the train but journeys back and forth by the hot-springs area of his memories.

The most famous hot springs in Tsugaru are Asamushi Hot Springs, perhaps, followed by Owani Hot Springs. Owani is close to the southern edge of Tsugaru and close to the prefectural boundary with Akita. More than hot springs, Tsugaru is known throughout Japan for its ski resorts. The hot springs are in the foothills of the mountains where the faint scent of the history of the Tsugaru clan lingers. My immediate family often came to this hot springs region to take the hot-spring cure. Although I also played there as a child, no memories as clear as those of Asamushi remain. I have many vivid memories of Asamushi but, at the same time, can't easily convey those memories. Nevertheless, my recollections of Owani are dear to me despite being hazy. Is it the difference between the sea and the mountains? I have not seen Owani Hot Springs for close to twenty years. Looking at it now, does it feel like a town ashamed of being given the leftovers of a city like Asamushi. I cannot give up on that town. Compared to Asamushi, traveling from Tokyo to Owani is a pain.

First of all, Owani is my last hope. The closest town to this hot springs is Ikarigaseki. It was a checkpoint between Tsugaru and Akita in the age of the former fief. Thus, this area has many historic landmarks. The way of life of the people of Tsugaru remains, has deep roots, and will not be

Introduction

easily brushed aside by city ways. Furthermore, the great last hope is Hirosaki Castle, which is seven miles north of here, and, even now, the castle tower remains. It is surrounded by cherry blossoms every spring and boasts of excellent health. I'd like to believe that as long as Hirosaki Castle remains, Owani Hot Springs will not sip the drippings of a city and descend into a drunken frenzy.

Hirosaki Castle lies at the center of the history of the Tsugaru clan. The founder of the Tsugaru clan, Oura Tamenobu, supported the Tokugawa clan in the Battle of Sekigahara. In Keicho year 8 (1603), by proclamation of the shogun Tokugawa Ieyasu, he became a noble with forty-seven thousand *koku* under the Tokugawa shogunate and immediately began to plot the boundary of the castle moat in Hirosaki-Takaoka. Hirosaki Castle was finally completed at the start of the reign of the second generation daimyo Tsugaru Nobuhira. Successive generations of daimyo were based in Hirosaki Castle. At the time of the fourth generation Nobumasa, Nobuhide was made to form a branch family in Kuroishi. The family was split into the two clans of Hirosaki and Kuroishi, and ruled Tsugaru. Despite Hidemasa's reputation gained in Tsugaru of the good governance and his being a star among the seven wise rulers of the Genroku era, which has been sung about, great famines during Houreki and Tenmei during the seventh generation Nobuyasu transformed all of Tsugaru into a gruesome hell. And the clan's finances plunged into extreme poverty. In the midst of dire prospects, the eight generation Nobuaki and the ninth generation Yasuchika desperately planned the restoration of the clan's power. At the time of the eleventh generation Yukitsugu, catastrophe had been narrowly avoided. In the age of the twelfth generation of Tsuguakira, the daimyo's fief was auspiciously restored to the emperor and gave

Introduction

birth to the present-day Aomori Prefecture. That is a brief overview of the circumstances of the history of Hirosaki Castle and the history of Tsugaru. I intend to describe more about Tsugaru's history later. For now, I will write a bit about my recollections of Hirosaki and tie them to this introduction of Tsugaru.

I spent three years in the castle town of Hirosaki. During those years, I studied the literature course at Hirosaki High School. At the time, I suspected the course mainly consisted of *gidayu* recitations for puppet theater. It was very strange. On the way home from school, I'd stop by the home of a woman teacher of gidayu. The first time, the puppet theater play was probably *The Diary of the Morning Glory* or something like that, I can't remember. Other plays like *The Village of Nozaki*, *Tsubozaka*, and *Kamiji* are burned into my memory. Why do I begin with something so strange and out of character? I don't think the full responsibility lies with the city of Hirosaki, but I'd like Hirosaki to accept a speck of responsibility.

Gidayu was mysteriously popular in this town. Sometimes amateurs held gidayu recitals in the town's theaters. Once, I went to listen, but the town patrons wore *kamishimo* ceremonial samurai dress and gave solemn recitations of the gidayu. Not one of them was adept but they spoke from their hearts without being the least bit pretentious and gave thoughtful recitations. From long ago, few men of refined taste seemed to inhabit Aomori City. However, they were cunning men who practiced the short love songs only to elicit, "Oh, you are so good," from the geisha or to use their refined behaviors as weapons of government and business policies. I think these pitiful patrons, who easily broke into heavy perspiration to study a vapid traditional art, often appear in Hirosaki City.

In other words, true dummies still live in Hirosaki. The

Introduction

following words are written in the ancient writings of war chronicles called *Eiki Gunki*.

> The hearts of the people of the two provinces of Mutsu and Dewa are foolish and do not know how to submit to a strongman. He becomes an enemy of the ancestors. He becomes vulgar. His strength simply came from the fortunes of war at the time. He boasts of power and influence but will not be obeyed.

The people of Hirosaki possess this truly foolish willpower and do not know how to bow to strongmen despite being defeated over and over. A defense of conceited aloofness tends to transform into a joke to the rest of the world.

Thanks to my three years there, I am struck by nostalgia and zealously watch gidayu. I express my romantic nature below. The following passages are from an old novel of mine but, I confess with a wry smile, they are only quirky fabrications.

> I have fond memories of drinking wine in a coffee shop. One time, I brazenly went to eat at a restaurant with a geisha. My younger self did not consider that to be particularly bad. I always believed behaving like a stylish yakuza was a lofty hobby. By going to eat two or three times at the quiet, old restaurant in the castle town, my instinct for style made heads snap up. Then I found my purpose. I wanted to dress in the clothes of the fireman seen in the play *The Quarrels of Megumi*, sit cross-legged in a tatami room overlooking the inner garden of the restaurant, and say things like, "My, my, you are too pretty today." Still enthused, I started to prepare my outfit.

Introduction

I shoved my hands in the big pocket of my dark blue workman's apron. An old-fashioned wallet was inside. When I walk with my arms folded in my kimono, I looked like a full-fledged yakuza. I also bought an obi sash. This sash made from Hakata cloth squeaked when tightened. I ordered an unlined kimono made of *tozan* cloth from the kimono shop. Unfortunately, these clothes were indecipherable. Was I a fireman? A professional gambler? A shop boy? They lacked a unifying theme. However, if my clothes gave the impression of a man who frequented the theater, I was satisfied. Summer began and I wore hemp sandals on my bare feet.

That was good, but a strange thought flashed through my mind. It was long underwear. I considered wearing long, formfitting, dark blue work pants like the fireman in the play. I was called, "Clown," and I rolled up the hem of my kimono ready to fight. At that time, the dark blue work pants looked so much better, like they pierced my eyes. Short underpants were forbidden. I tried to buy the work pants and ran around from one end of the castle town to the other but found none.

I'd breathlessly explain, "You know, what plasterers wear. Do you have those tight, dark blue work pants?" I asked at dry goods shops and *tabi* sock shops, but the shop workers smiled and shook their heads no. It was already hot, and sweat poured out of me as I ran around on my quest. Finally, the proprietor of one shop said, "We don't carry them, but there's a specialty shop for firefighters in the alley around the corner. Go ask there. They may have them." Of course. Firefighting never crossed my mind.

A shop for firefighters made sense, and I sped to that shop in the alley. Large and small firefighting pumps were lined up in the shop. Clothes were displayed, too. I felt helpless, but my courage was inspired. I asked if they had work pants, the prompt response was yes. They were dark blue, cotton work pants, but thick, red stripes ran down both sides of the pants to indicate a fireman. I didn't have the courage to walk around in them and, sadly, had to abandon the work pants.

Even at the home of stupidity, there is little of this level of stupidity. As I copied this passage, I sunk into a little melancholy. The red-light district where the restaurant I dined with the geisha stood was probably Enoki Alley. This event happened nearly twenty years ago and has faded from memory. I do remember Enoki Alley at the foot of Omiyasaka Hill. The area I walked around drenched in sweat to buy dark blue work pants was the most lively shopping district of the castle town and called Dote-machi. In comparison, the red-light district in Aomori is called Hama-machi. That name is missing a personality. The shopping district in Aomori corresponding to Dote-machi in Hirosaki is Oo-machi. I feel the same about that name. Next, I will list the names of towns in Hirosaki beside those in Aomori. The differences in the personalities of these two small cities become stark. The names of towns in Hirosaki are Hon-cho, Zaifu-cho, Dote-machi, Sumiyoshi-cho, Okeya-machi, Douya-machi, Chabatake-cho, Daikan-cho, Kaya-cho, Hyakkoku-machi, Kamisayashi-machi, Shimosayashi-machi, Teppou-machi, Wakadou-cho, Kobito-cho, Takajou-machi, Gojitsukoku-machi, and Konya-machi [Capital Town, Government Town, Embankment Town, Good Living Town, Cooper Town, Coppersmith Town, Tea Field Town, Locally Administrated Town, Silvergrass Town, One Hundred Stones Town, Upper Sword Sheather Town, Lower Sword Sheather Town, Gun Town, Foot Soldier Town, Dwarf

Introduction

Town, Falconer Town, Fifty Stones Town, and Dyer Town]. In contrast, the names of the towns in Aomori are Hama-machi, Shin Hama-machi, Oo-machi, Kome-machi, Shin-machi, Yanagi-machi, Tera-machi, Tsutsumi-machi, Shio-machi, Shijimi-machi, Shin Shijimi-machi, Ura-machi, Namiuchi, and Sakae-machi [Beach Town, New Beach Town, Big Town, Rice Town, New Town, Willow Town, Shrine Town, Embankment Town, Salt Town, Clam Town, New Clam Town, Inlet Town, Shoreline Town, and Prosperous Town].

However, I never thought of Hirosaki City as the superior town and Aomori City as the inferior town. Old-fashioned names like Takajou-machi and Konya-machi are not unique to Hirosaki but towns bearing those kinds of names are found in castle towns throughout Japan. Of course, Mount Iwaki in Hirosaki is more beautiful than the Hakkoda Mountains in Aomori. But the master novelist from Tsugaru, Kasai Zenzou, gave this lesson to this junior author from his native land, "Don't be conceited. Mount Iwaki looks magnificent because no high mountains surround it. Go to other countries and look around. A mountain like that is commonplace. With no high mountains in the area, it appears blessed. Don't be vain."

Although countless historic castle towns are spread throughout Japan, for some reason, the inhabitants of the castle town of Hirosaki seem to take pride in the feudal nature of their stubbornness. This is not defiance, but compared to Kyushu, Shikoku, and Yamato, the Tsugaru region can be said to be almost entirely a frontier. What kind of history is there to be proud of throughout the province? During the recent Meiji Restoration, what kind of loyalists emerged from this clan? What was the clan's attitude? To be blunt, wasn't their course of action to merely follow the lead of the other clans? Exactly where is this proud tradition? What is the source of the stubborn swagger of the people of Hirosaki?

A man with power was no good. He had pride in power that came from very good luck. I heard when His Excellency Ichinohe Hyoe, the general who hailed from this region, returned home, he always wore serge hakama trousers when wearing Japanese clothes. If he returned home wearing military dress, the people of his hometown would glare at him in anger, square their elbows, and wonder aloud what he had turned into because, at best, he had a stroke of very good luck. Wisely, when he returned home, he wore serge hakama trousers with his Japanese-style clothes. While not entirely true, this fable is plausible because the inhabitants of the castle town of Hirosaki have a baffling vicious rebelliousness.

What is being hidden? The truth is I have a bone with that kind of bad behavior in my body, too. That's not the only reason, but thanks to that bad bone, I am unable to rise above living day and night in the attic of a tenement house. Several years ago, a magazine company solicited me to write for *A Few Words to My Hometown*. My answer was *I love you, I hate you*.

I have slandered Hirosaki. However, this does not arise from a hatred of Hirosaki but is a reflection of me, the author. I am a native of Tsugaru. Generations of my ancestors were farmers in the Tsugaru clan. In other words, I am a pureblood native of Tsugaru. Thus, I badmouth Tsugaru holding little back. If a native of another land heard my ridicule and was prompted to underestimate Tsugaru, of course, that would trouble me. No matter what I say, I love Tsugaru.

Today, Hirosaki has ten thousand households and a population exceeding fifty thousand. Hirosaki Castle and the Five-Storied Pagoda of Saishoin Temple are desig-

Introduction

nated as national treasures. Tayama Katai praised Hirosaki Park as the finest in Japan when the cherry blossoms are in bloom. The headquarters of the Hirosaki Division are located there. The mountain pilgrimage *Oyama-sankei* takes place every year over three days, July 28 to August 1. Tens of thousands make the pilgrimage to the festival held at the rear shrine on top of the sacred Mount Iwaki in Tsugaru and pass through this very prosperous town while dancing all the way there and back. That's pretty much what is written in travel guides. Nonetheless, I've limited my descriptions of Hirosaki City to complaints.

Therefore, I traced the memories of my youth and wanted to depict a Hirosaki that lived up to its reputation. But each and every memory was silly, and I didn't get far. Unexpected abuse escaped from me, and I didn't know what to do. I'm too particular about this castle town of the former Tsugaru clan. Although this place should be the foundation of the quintessential spirit of a Tsugaru native, the character of this castle town remains vague in my description.

A castle tower surrounded by cherry blossoms is not unique to Hirosaki Castle. Aren't most of the castles in Japan surrounded by cherry blossoms? Isn't Owani Hot Springs able to preserve the scent of Tsugaru because it faces a side of the castle tower surrounded by cherry blossoms? Earlier I intended to write with foolish elation that Owani Hot Springs will not slurp up the drippings of the city and fall into a drunken frenzy as long as it faces Hirosaki Castle. I had an assortment of thoughts, but I sensed they were the sloppy sentimentality of the author's ornate prose. With nothing to rely on, I lost heart. In the end, this castle town is lackadaisical. Despite being the castle of generations of feudal lords, its prefectural authority was stolen by another up-and-coming town.

Introduction

Throughout Japan, most prefectural capitals are the castle towns of the former clans. However, the prefectural authority of Aomori Prefecture is not Hirosaki City but was moved to Aomori City. I believe even Aomori Prefecture was unhappy. I don't especially hate Aomori City. Witnessing the prosperity of a rising town is invigorating. While Hirosaki City was defeated, I lost patience with its apathy. The desire to support the loser is human nature.

Some way or another, I want to be on the side of Hirosaki City. Although my composition is poor, I struggled to devise different ways to write but was unable to describe the ultimate merits of Hirosaki and the power of Hirosaki Castle's uniqueness. I will say it again. This place is the foundation of the spirit of the people of Tsugaru. There should be something. There should be a brilliant tradition found nowhere else after a search of all Japan. I have an inkling of what it is, but in what form can I express it? I'm frustrated and annoyed by my inability to reveal this to the reader.

I was a literature student at Hirosaki High School and remember visiting Hirosaki Castle by myself at twilight one spring day. As I stood on the corner of the castle plot and gazed at Mount Iwaki, I was overcome with the horror of the realization that a land of dreams was silently expanding at my feet. Until then, I only thought that Hirosaki Castle was isolated from the town of Hirosaki. But right below the castle, a quaint town I never noticed before consisted of rows of small buildings, which kept the same form for a long time, for hundreds of years. I quieted my breath and squatted down. Oh, so there's also a town here. The young me felt like I was looking at a dream and a deep sigh escaped. I sensed the *hidden pool* that often appears in the verses of the *Man'yoshu*. Why did I feel I understood Hirosaki and Tsugaru at that moment? I

Introduction

thought Hirosaki was no ordinary town as long as this town existed. The reader may not understand my conceited conclusion. Hirosaki Castle is a rare, famous castle because of this hidden pool. And now I have no choice but to push through.

When the flowers on the many branches open near the hidden pool, and the castle tower with white walls stands silently, the castle is, without a doubt, a famous castle of this world. For all eternity, the hot springs beside the famous castle may never lose their rustic, simple character. In today's words, I could try *optimistic outlook* as my parting words to my beloved Hirosaki Castle. Come to think of it, similar to the grueling task of describing my relatives, describing the heart of my hometown is no easy task.

I don't know whether to praise or to criticize. In this introduction to Tsugaru, as I developed the memories of my youth about Kanagi, Goshogawara, Aomori, Hirosaki, Asamushi, and Owani, my jumbled words are a collection of blasphemous criticisms by someone who doesn't know his place. As expected, I puzzled over how to accurately tell the stories of these six towns and, naturally, became depressed. I may spew violent words that deserve capital punishment.

These six towns were most dear to me in my past, fashioned my personality, and determined my destiny. On the other hand, I may have blind spots regarding them. I realized I am in no way the best person to tell the stories of these towns. In the main story, I will try to avoid writing about these six towns and write about other towns in Tsugaru.

Finally, I can return to the opening paragraph of this introduction with "I spent three weeks one spring touring the Tsugaru Peninsula at the northern end of Honshu." By taking this trip, I saw other towns and villages of Tsugaru

Introduction

for the first time in my life. Until then, I knew nothing about any towns other than the six I mentioned. In grammar school, I went on several field trips near Kanagi. Today, those fond memories are lost to me.

During midsummer vacations while in middle school, I lay on a couch in the Western-style room on the second floor of my house and guzzle cider as I randomly read my way through my older brothers' book collections and never went on any trips. During my vacations while in high school, I always visited the home in Tokyo of my next oldest brother (he was studying sculpture, but died at twenty-seven years old). When I graduated from high school, I went to college in Tokyo. For the next ten years, I never returned to my hometown; therefore, I must say this trip to Tsugaru was a momentous event.

I want to avoid having the know-it-all opinions resembling an expert about the topology, geology, astronomy, politics, history, education, and hygiene of the towns and villages I saw on this trip. I say this, but in the end, I have an embarrassingly thin veneer of one night of study. Those of you interested in these topics should pay close attention to specialists in those fields. I have another specialty. For the time being, the world may call that subject love. This subject researches the touching of the heart of one person to the heart of another. On this trip, my investigation will focus on this subject. Regardless of the perspective taken in this investigation, if I'm able to convey life today in Tsugaru to the reader, I probably won't receive a passing grade as a record of the culture and geography of Tsugaru during the Showa era but will have found success.

1

THE PILGRIMAGE

"**Now, why are** you going on this trip?"
"I'm having problems."
"As usual, I can't believe you're having problems, even a little."
"Masaoka Shiki, thirty-six; Ozaki Koyo, thirty-seven; Saito Ryoku, thirty-eight; Kunikida Doppo, thirty-eight; Nagatsuka Takashi, thirty-seven; Akutagawa Ryunosuke, thirty-six; Kamura Isota, thirty-seven."
"What's your point?"
"They died at those ages. They dropped dead one after another. I'm creeping toward that age. To a writer, this is the most important age."
"So what's bothering you?"
"What are you saying? Stop joking. You're supposed to have a little understanding. I will say no more. If I speak, I will be showing off. Anyway, I'm going on this trip."

Aging well may be to blame or my belief that explaining my feelings was smug, but I didn't want to say anything (also because it's mostly trite literary flashiness).

A while ago, a friendly editor at a publishing house

asked me to write about Tsugaru. While I'm alive, I want to explore each corner of the region of my birth and, one spring, left Tokyo looking like a beggar.

This event occurred in the middle of May. Describing myself as a beggar may be subjective. However, I am being objective when I say I did not look very stylish. I don't own one business suit. I only wear the work clothes of a laborer. And these clothes weren't made by a tailor on special order. These clothes are baffling, unfamiliar work clothes resembling jackets and pants made from scraps of cotton cloth laying around and dyed dark blue by someone in the house. Right after dying, the cloth was supposed to be dark blue, but after I wore them once or twice, they faded into a strange color resembling purple.

With the exception of a stunning woman, purple Western-style clothes are not flattering. I added green gaiters made of a staple fiber and rubber-soled, white canvas shoes. My hat was a tennis hat also made from a staple fiber. The dandy dressed like that went on a trip for the first time in his life. Surprisingly, a *haori* coat with an embroidered crest sewn in as a memento of my mother, a lined Oshima kimono, and Sendaihira hakama trousers were hidden in my backpack. I have no idea when any of those clothes would be worn.

I boarded the express train leaving Ueno at 5:30 pm. As the night grew late, I shivered from the cold. Beneath my jacket-like clothing, I only wore two thin shirts. Under my pants, I only wore underpants. Even people wearing winter coats and prepared with lap blankets were cold and whining about the strange chill of that night. I hadn't expected the bitter cold. In Tokyo at that time, impatient people were already walking around wearing unlined serge kimonos.

I had forgotten about the cold of Tohoku. My hands

and feet shriveled and I shrunk like a turtle. I tried to convince myself this is an exercise for training my mind. Dawn finally came and it was cold. I gave up training my mind. We would soon arrive in Aomori. I entered the lowly state of fervently wishing for the realistic circumstance of wanting to sit cross-legged beside a fireside in an inn somewhere and drink hot sake. We arrived in Aomori at eight in the morning. My friend T was at the station to welcome me. I posted a letter to him beforehand.

"I thought you'd be wearing Japanese clothes," he said.

"This is a different age," I tried hard to joke.

T brought a little girl with him. The thought, A present for her would have been nice, sprung to mind.

"Why don't you come home with me and rest for a while?"

"Thanks. I'm thinking about going to N's home in Kanita by noon today."

"I know, N told me and is probably waiting for you. Well, you're welcome to rest at my home until the bus leaves for Kanita."

My vulgar but cherished wish to sit cross-legged beside the hearth drinking hot sake was miraculously coming true. At T's home, a charcoal fire was blazing in the hearth, and a bottle of sake rested in an iron kettle.

"You've had a long journey," said T and bowed to me again, "How about a beer?"

"No, thanks. The sake is fine," I said clearing my throat.

In the old days, T lived at my house and mostly took care of the chicken coops. We were the same age and became good friends. In those days, I remember hearing my grandmother criticize T with "Yelling at the maids has good and bad points." Later T went to Aomori to study and then worked in a hospital in Aomori City and gained the trust of both the patients and the hospital employees. A few years ago, he went to war to fight on an isolated island in the south but got sick and returned home last year. After he recovered, he began to work at the hospital.

"What was your happiest time on the battlefield?"

T's response was swift.

"That was when I filled my cup to the brim with my beer rations on the battlefield. I sipped with great care and thought about taking the cup away from my lips for a rest, but the cup never left my lips. Never."

T was also a man who liked sake. However, he didn't even drink a little with me and from time to time lightly coughed.

"How are you feeling?" I asked.

Sometime in the past, T had a lung problem that flared up again on the battlefield.

"This time I'm serving on the home front. When caring for patients in the hospital, if you haven't suffered once from sickness, you lack understanding. Now, I have good experience."

"It seems you've become an adult. In reality, it's the chest illness," I said. I got tipsy and began to shamelessly expound on medicine to a doctor.

"Your disease is in your mind. If you forget about it, you will recover. And drink a lot of sake once in a while."

"Oh, well, I'm not overdoing it," he said smiling. My reckless medical science could hardly be relied on by professionals.

"Would you like something to eat? Around this time of the year, delicious fish are scarce even in Aomori."

"No, thank you," I said while gazing at the trays on the side, "Everything looks delicious. Don't go to any trouble. I don't want to eat too much."

I made one promise to myself before setting off to

Tsugaru. I would be indifferent to food. I'm not comfortable saying I'm not much of a saint, but the people of Tokyo are greedy for food. I'm a stodgy man or a samurai who revels in honorable poverty by chewing on a toothpick as if he just finished a meal. But I love being amused by my idiotic stoicism that hinted of desperation.

I thought about using that post-meal toothpick, but that sort of manly pride tends to look ridiculous. Among the Tokyoites who go to the provinces lacking spirit and will, most will not die of starvation but will exaggerate and complain about their horrible plight. After the meal of white rice held out by the country people is presented and eaten, I've heard rumors of someone wearing a servile smile and full of flattery ask, "Is there any more to eat? Is this a potato? Thank you. It's been many months since I've eaten a potato this delicious. I'd like to take a little home, if you could slice it up for me…"

Everyone in Tokyo receives identical food rations. It's a miracle for only that person to be in a state of near starvation. Perhaps, they underwent gastric dilation, but the plea for food is disgraceful. Each and every time, without saying in defiance words like "For the sake of the country," they must hold on to their pride as human beings. A few exceptions in Tokyo go to the countryside and complain irresponsibly about a shortage of food in the imperial capital. I also heard rumors that the people in the countryside scorn guests from Tokyo who come to beg for food.

I didn't come to Tsugaru to scrounge for food. Although I looked like a purple beggar, I was a truthful and loving beggar and not a polished-rice beggar! In order to be the glory of all the people of Tokyo, I hid my determination to cut out the pretentious attitude in the tone of my voice. If someone looked at me and said, "This is rice. Please eat until your stomach bursts. Is the situation horrible in Tokyo?" Even if they said it with kindness from their hearts, I would only eat a little. I imagined I would say, "I'm used to it. Tokyo's rice is delicious. When I think the side dishes were almost gone, more rations come. Without my noticing, my stomach shrinks, so I'm full after eating a little. It happens a lot."

However, this warped caution of mine was pointless. I visited the homes of friends here and there in Tsugaru. Not one said to me, "Here's some rice. Please eat until your belly bursts." My eighty-eight-year-old grandmother at my parents' home, in particular, looking ashamed said, "Since Tokyo probably has all sorts of delicious food, it would be hard to find something delicious for you to eat. Why would you want to be forced to eat pickled melons? These days, there are almost no sake lees." I was actually happy.

In other words, I only met gentle people who were not sensitive to things like food. I thanked god for my luck. No one said, "Please, take this. Please, take that," and persisted in pushing food gifts on me. Thankfully, I continued my pleasant journey carrying a lightweight backpack. However, when I returned to Tokyo, I was surprised to find small parcels sent from the amazing people at each place I visited before returning home. I digress, but T never recommended food to me, and the state of food in Tokyo never came up. We mainly talked about our memories of the times spent together at my home in Kanagi.

"I think of you as my close friend."

My words were conceited and filled with the theatricality of outrage, rudeness, and sarcasm. I squirm at having said that. Was there no other way to say that?

"But you're uncomfortable." T made a perceptive guess.

He said, "I worked at your home in Kanagi, so you're my boss. If you don't think so, I would not be happy. It's strange. Although twenty years have passed, even now, I constantly dream of your house in Kanagi. I even saw it on the battlefield. I forgot to feed the chickens. Dammit! I thought and instantly woke from the dream."

The time for the bus came. I went out with T. The weather was no longer cold but pleasant, and I drank hot sake. Was it cold? Sweat stained my forehead. We talked about the cherry blossoms in Gappo Park being in full bloom. The streets of Aomori City were dry and white. No, I will be prudent in my explanation of the nonsensical impression reflected on my drunken eyes. Today, Aomori City is zealous about shipbuilding. We hurried to the bus depot, but along the way, I visited the grave of Papa Toyoda, who had been so kind to me during my middle school years.

The old me would have asked, "Why don't we both go to Kanita?" without a care in the world. But as I aged, I remember to be a little more reserved. No, my feelings are hard to explain. In other words, we have grown up. Being grown is miserable. Despite sharing mutual affection, we must show discretion and preserve good manners with others.

Why is so much discretion required? There is no answer because too much treachery and humiliation abound. The discovery that people are treacherous is the first theme when a youth moves into adulthood. An adult is a youth who has been backstabbed. We walked without speaking until T said, "I'll go to Kanita tomorrow. I'll take the first bus tomorrow morning and drop by N's house."

"What about the hospital?"

"Tomorrow is Sunday."

"Oh, really? You could have said so sooner."

Traces of our foolish youth remained.

2

KANITA

The Tokai coast of the Tsugaru Peninsula was a prosperous shipping route long called Sotogahama. I boarded the bus in Aomori City and headed north along the Tokai coast, passed through villages and towns like Ushirogata, Yomogita, Kanita, Tairadate, Ippongi, Imabetsu and arrived at the famed Minmaya from the legend of Yoshitsune. The trip took about four hours.

Minmaya was the last stop of the bus line. I would walk north along the narrow road from Minmaya at the water's edge for almost three hours to the hamlet of Tappi. As the name, where the dragon flies, says, this place is where the road runs out. The cape is the northern tip of Honshu. However, recently, this area has become very important for defense; therefore, I must avoid mentioning the number of miles and other particulars. The belt of Sotogahama boasts the oldest history in Tsugaru.

Kanita is the largest hamlet in Sotogahama. From Aomori City by bus, they say the ride via Ushirogata and Yomogita lasts about ninety minutes, but I reached this town, that is, the center of Sotogahama, in about two hours. There are close to one thousand households and a population larger than five thousand. The recently built Kanita Police Station stands out as the most eye-catching of the buildings passed by the Sotogahama line.

Kanita, Yomogita, Tairadate, Ippongi, Imabetsu, and Minmaya, namely all of the Sotogahama hamlets, are under the jurisdiction of this police station. According to *A Brief History of Aomori Prefecture* published by Takeuchi Umpei, a native of Hirosaki, long ago, sand iron was produced at the beach at Kanita. Today, it's no longer produced, but the construction of Hirosaki Castle in the Keicho era used refined sand from this beach. During the uprising of the Ainu people in Kanbun year 9 (1669), five large ships to suppress the rebellion were built on the Kanita beach. During the Genroku era, the fourth daimyo Tsugaru Nobumasa designated Kanita harbor as one of the six harbors and three checkpoint stations that together formed the Tsugaru Kuura and placed the town magistrate there. It primarily managed timber exports, but I learned all of this through later research. At the time, I only knew Kanita was famous for producing crabs and N, my only friend from middle school, lived there.

In this walking tour of Tsugaru, I wanted to stop by N's home and spend a pleasant time. I sent a letter to N before I came and wrote something like:

> Please, don't go to any trouble. Act like you know nothing. Please don't hold any kind of reception. Well, just apple cider and crabs are fine.

The only exception to my self-discipline regarding food is crabs.

I love crabs. Why do I love them? I love crabs, shrimp, squilla, only foods with no nutrients. Therefore, my favorite is sake. A disciple of love and truth who is supposed to have no interest in food talking like this has, by chance, exposed one edge of my innate greed.

At N's home in Kanita, crabs were piled on a large tray with red cabriole legs and carried to me.

"Do you have to drink apple cider? Are both Japanese sake and beer bad?" asked N with difficulty.

I know about their bad parts and decided they were better than cider, but the *grown-up* me knew the valuable parts of Japanese sake and beer. I held back when I wrote apple cider in the letter. I heard that these days in the Tsugaru district, apple cider is fairly abundant like wine in Koushu.

"Either is fine," I said with a confused smile.

N looked relieved and said, "I feel better hearing that. I don't like cider. The truth is, my wife saw your letter and said Dazai has given up drinking sake and beer in Tokyo and wants to drink the apple cider of home. Because you definitely wrote this in your letter, we should serve you cider. But I couldn't, I told her you don't hate beer or sake and, out of character, you were acting reserved."

"Well, your wife was not wrong."

"What are you saying? Come here. First, we'll have sake? Beer?"

"Later is better for beer," I said a bit shamelessly.

"I think so too. Hey, bring the sake! If warm is okay with you, she'll bring it now."

> It is hard to forget sake from
>   anywhere.
> Speak of a land far from home,
>   renew an old friendship.
> Together, we did not reach greatness
>   and were surprised by gray hair.

> Parted twenty years ago. Traveled
> more than three thousand *ri*.
> Now, without a cup of sake, life
> cannot be described.
>
> Haku Kyoi

During my middle school years, I never went to play at anyone's home. The reason was I often went to play at my classmate N's home. In those days, N boarded on the second floor of a large sake dealer in Tera-machi. Every morning, we met and walked to school together. And on the way home, we took our time walking along the coast on the back streets. Even when it rained, we weren't in a rush and walked at a leisurely pace even if we ended up soaked like wet rats. Thinking about it now, we were two dopey kids with generous spirits. That might have been the key to our friendship.

We ran around and played tennis in a large field in front of the temple and, on Sundays, carried *bento* boxes to play at a nearby mountain. The *friend* who appeared in my first novella *Memories* was based on this friend N. After graduating from middle school, N left for Tokyo and worked at a magazine company. I was a few years behind N in leaving for Tokyo to enroll in college. At that time, we renewed our friendship. N was boarding in Ikebukuro, and I boarded in Takadanobaba, and we saw each other almost every day.

This time our fun wasn't tennis and running. N left the magazine company to work at an insurance company. Like me, his big-hearted nature led to him always being cheated by people. Each time someone cheated me, I became a little darker and meaner. In contrast, N became more easy-going and light-hearted, no matter how much he was cheated. N is a mysterious man and admirable for not feeling mistreated. His flippant friend considers that to be a benefit inherited from his ancestors and holds his gentle nature in high regard.

N visited me at my birthplace in Kanagi during middle school. Even after coming to Tokyo, he often visited the home of my next-older brother in Tokka. When this brother died at twenty-seven, N took off work to do various errands for me and was thanked by all of my relatives. Later, N had to return to the countryside to take over his family's rice polishing business. He gained the trust of the young people of the village due to his mysterious innate virtue after inheriting the family business. A few years ago, he was elected as a town councilman of Kanita, took on various responsibilities of executive secretary of some association, and became an indispensable man in Kanita.

That evening, a couple of people stopped by the home of N, a young influential man in the district, for drinks of sake and beer. N's popularity was amazing, the star of the troupe. What was told to the world as the rules of a pilgrimage by the elderly Basho, the first condition was to not drink sake for enjoyment, to refuse treats of food and drink, to prevent becoming even slightly intoxicated, and to never end up confused. However, I understand the advice from the *Analects of Confucius* says to drink unknown quantities of sake without acting rude. I did not follow the teachings of Basho.

It's all right to be dead drunk as long as you aren't rude. Isn't that obvious? I can hold my alcohol. I think I may be many times stronger than the old man Basho. I don't intend to be stupid and get too drunk at someone else's home. If not given a cup of sake, I can't be normal. I drink a lot. Another rule of a pilgrimage of Basho is there should be no small talk only haiku, and if small talk starts, you should work hard to doze off. I didn't follow this rule either.

From our perspective as laymen, as much as we'd like to suspect the pilgrimage of Basho was not a business trip to the countryside to publicize the correct style of haiku, he held haiku gatherings at each destination of the trip and set up regional branches for advancing the proper style of haiku. If a lecturer is surrounded by special students of haiku, the students avoid small talk with each other. If small talk starts, what should you do? Pretend to be asleep? My trip is not a trip to set up regional branches in the style of Dazai. N wanted to hear a lecture on literature from me and had no reason to throw a party. Also, influential men were the visitors at N's home that night. Because I have been a close friend of N for many years, they felt somewhat friendly to me, too, and we exchanged drinks. I took the offensive and explained the location of the literary mind every way possible. When engaged in small talk with the alcove post at my back, I believed faking sleep would not be a gentle gesture.

That night, I did not speak one word about literature. I didn't even use the words of Tokyo. I struggled to not act prim and spoke in a pure Tsugaru dialect. I only chatted about trivial everyday matters. Not working too hard to that point was good. As much as I thought anyone at the party was sure to feel left out, I faced these people as the jerky younger brother from the Tsushima family in Tsugaru. (The name Tsushima Shuji was my name entered in the family registry at birth. The kanji for Uncle Scum could be used for the one called the jerky brother. If the third or the fourth son is spoken of with disdain, those words are used in the dialect of this region.) For this trip, I had no reason not to be reduced again to this Uncle Scum of the Tsushima. They felt uneasy towards me as a city boy and desired to grab onto me as a native of Tsugaru.

In other words, I wanted to understand the nature of a Tsugaru native and embarked on this trip. I came to Tsugaru to search for a purebred Tsugaru native to model my life on. I easily discovered him everywhere. It didn't matter who. Arrogant criticism by an indigent traveler cannot be allowed. That is extremely rude. He would not be discovered in the actions and words of individuals or in the hospitality extended to me. I intended not to travel with the wary eyes of a detective. So I mostly looked down at my feet as I walked. I often heard my fate being whispered in my ears. I believed it. I discovered it was very subjective with neither reason or form. I didn't worry particularly about who did what or what someone said. That was natural because I have almost no capacity to fret about anything. In fact, I saw nothing. I wrote the strange saying, "There is reality in belief, and reality can never be what people are made to believe," twice in my travel journal.

Although prudent, my description left a bad impression. My theory is confused. I often don't understand what I'm saying. And I lie. Thus, I hate explaining my feelings. I only blush red with shame like it's all transparent affectation. Although I know I will feel deep regret, I get excited and pout giving my mouth whiplash and slurring my words and begin a long-winded, incoherent complaint. My sad fate may be that contempt will develop in my companion's heart or feelings of mercy will be awakened.

That night, without exposing that bad impression, I rebelled against the teachings of Basho and took an interest only in small talk without dozing off. Gazing at the mountain of crabs before my eyes, I drank until late in the night. N's petite and wise wife noticed I enjoyed only looking at the mountain of crabs but never reached for one. She thought I had tired of shelling crabs and, with great skill, diligently shelled them herself and piled the beautiful white meat on each crab shell. Several fruits were offered to me in the form of a fragrant, refreshing jelly dessert containing fruits in their original forms.

Perhaps, the crabs were brought from Kanita beach that morning. The flavor was fresh and light like freshly-picked fruit. I remained tranquil as I broke my self-discipline of apathy towards food and ate three or four. That night, N's wife gave a tray to each guest, even the local people were surprised by the abundance of food on those trays.

After the prominent guests went home, N and I moved the drinking party from the inner drawing room to the parlor, and the *second wind* began. In the Tsugaru region, after the guests leave after a gathering at someone's home for a celebration, the second wind is a modest thank-you party where a small number of relatives and close friends gathers the leftover snacks for drinking and sounds like the word meaning insatiable drinker in the Tsugaru dialect. N was a stronger drinker than I, and the danger of slipping into a disturbance wouldn't happen with us.

"And you..." I sighed deeply and said, "always drink. But since you were my teacher, it won't be a problem."

In fact, N taught me to drink. That is certain.

"Okay," said N with a cup in hand. He looked grim and nodded.

"I think about that often. You seem to have a fondness for using sake in an attempt to fail. I feel responsible for this, and it's hard on me. These days, I'm struggling to reconsider this. Even if I had not taught you, you're definitely the type of guy who, all by yourself, would have become a sake drinker. That's not my business."

"Ah, that's true. That's exactly right. You're not the least bit responsible. You're absolutely right."

Soon his wife came in and we chatted about our children. As the second wind quietly progressed, crowing cocks announced dawn to our surprise, and I withdrew to my bedroom.

When I woke the next day, I heard the voice of T from Aomori City. As promised, he came on the first bus of the morning. I leaped to my feet. With T here, I felt calm and reassured. T brought along a co-worker from the Aomori hospital who was fond of novels and a man named S, the business manager at the Kanita branch hospital of the Aomori hospital. While washing my face, I heard the young man M, who liked novels, was from Imabetsu near Minmaya and tagged along with a bashful smile. N told me about him when I was in Kanita. M seemed to be an old friend of N, T, and S. After a short discussion, we settled on going cherry-blossom viewing in the mountains near Kanita.

We set off to Kanranzan. I wore my customary purple jacket and green gaiters. My garish outfit was not needed. The mountain was a small one no more than one hundred meters high and beside the town of Kanita. However, the view from this mountain was not bad. On that fine day with almost no wind, we could see Natsudomari Cape across Aomori Bay and Shimokita Peninsula, which looked very close, separated from us by Tairadate Strait.

People in the south may imagine the seas in Tohoku as dark, threatening, raging waters. The seas near Kanita are tranquil with light-colored water, a low salt content, and the faint scent of a beach. Snow melts into the sea making it similar to a lake. For reasons of national defense, its depth and other aspects are best left unsaid. The waves gently lap the sandy beach. Over the four seasons, nets are erected close to the seaside, and crabs, shrimp, various fish like flounder, mackerel, sardines, cod, and monkfish are easily caught.

Today as in the past in this town, every morning, fish are piled into carts. Fish sellers walk around and sound mad as they shout, "Mackerel over shrimp! Greens over mackerel! Mackerel over sea perch! They walk around selling local fish caught that day not the unsold leftovers from the previous day, maybe those fish are sent elsewhere.

Therefore, the townspeople eat only fish caught live the same day. However, on days with no fish caught because of turbulent seas, not one fresh fish can be found in town. On those days, the townspeople eat dried food and wild plants. Not only Kanita, any fishing village in the Sotogahama belt, and not only Sotogahama, any fishing village on the west coast of Tsugaru is the same. Kanita is also blessed with amazing wild plants.

Kanita is a town on the coast but lies both on the plain and in the mountains. On the Tokai coast of the Tsugaru Peninsula, the mountains are near the coast. The plain is meager, and some rice and crop fields were reclaimed on the mountain slopes. Over the mountain, the people living on the expansive Tsugaru Plain on the western part of the Tsugaru Peninsula call the people of the Sotogahama region *The Shadows* because they live in the shadows of the mountains and are not inclined towards pity.

However, only the Kanita region has splendid fertile plains that are in no way inferior to the western region. If pitied by the people in the west, the people in Kanita are tickled. In the Kanita area, a gentle river called the Kanita River flows slowly and discharges rich waters. The rice and crop fields expand widely over the river basin. This area is battered by strong winds from the east and the west, and years of crop failures are not few. However, the land is not as infertile as the people in the west imagine.

When looking down from Kanranzan, Kanita River with abundant waters undulated like a long snake. We had a wonderful view of the rich, paddy fields planted first on both sides of the river and quietly waiting. The mountains are the Bonju mountain range, a branch of the Ou mountain range that goes directly north from the root of the Tsugaru Peninsula, runs to Cape Tappi at the tip of the peninsula, and drops to the sea.

Mount Okuratake consists of small mountains two hundred to three or four hundred meters high and towers in blue almost directly west of Kanranzan. It is one of the highest mountains in this mountain range along with Mount Masukawatake and may be seven hundred meters high. But don't judge a book by its cover. Because the people of Tsugaru are utilitarian, not afraid to be declared killjoys, they see no need to be ashamed of the low mountain range. This range is the leading habitat of *hiba* cypress in all Japan. The product of Tsugaru with a proud, long tradition is cypress, not apples.

Varieties of apples were received from Americans in the first year of Meiji (1868) and test planted. Later, in Meiji year 20, a French pruning method taught by a French missionary led to sudden success. From then on, the people in the region began to cultivate apples. The products known throughout the country as specialty products of Aomori after entering the Taisho era are not silly novelty products like Tokyo *Kaminari Okoshi* rice cakes or *Kuwana* grilled food, but compared to mandarin oranges from Kishu, have a very shallow history.

The people of Kanto and Kansai immediately think of apples when they hear Tsugaru and appear not to know about the cypress trees. I believe those trees are the origin of the name of the prefecture Aomori (green forests). In the mountains of Tsugaru, the branches of the trees intertwine and even winter is a lush green.

Since long ago, it has been counted as one of the three largest forests in Japan. From the Showa year 4 (1929) edition of the *Japan Geography and Customs Survey*:

> First, the large forests in Tsugaru are linked to unfinished work of the founder Tsugaru Tamenobu at his death. Under the strict system in effect since that time, those luxuriant forests still exist and comprise the model forest system of our nation. Beginning in the Tenna and Jokyo eras (1681-1688), trees were planted over several dozen miles of sand dunes on Japan Sea coast as an investment to block sea breezes and cultivate wilderness in the downstream area of the Iwaki River. Since that time, the clan attacked that plan and worked earnestly to reforest. As a result, the mature trees of the so-called Byobu forest were seen in the Kan'ei era (1624-1644), and the cultivation of eight thousand three hundred hectares of arable land was seen. And the lands in the clan domain often underwent forestation and provided the large forests at over one hundred locations for the clan. Even at the onset of the Meiji era (1868-1912), the authorities heeded forest management and heard about the popularity of the cypress trees in Aomori Prefecture. Timber from this region is well suited as wood for use in various buildings and has the property of water resistance. The timber yield is abundant, relatively easy to transport, and valued at eight hundred thousand koku.

These data are from the Showa year 4 edition, so the current yield may be three times greater.

Above I described cypress forests throughout the entire

Tsugaru region, but this alone cannot be the unique pride of only the Kanita area. The mountains thick with forests seen from Kanranzan are a belt of superior forests even for the Tsugaru region. A large picture of the mouth of Kanita River was published in the *Japan Geography and Customs Survey*. The caption for that picture said:

> There are national cypress forests dubbed the three most beautiful forests in Japan near Kanita River. Kanita is prosperous as a shipping port. From here, the logging railroad leaves the coast, enters the mountains, is piled with a great deal of wood everyday, and carries the load back here. Wood from this area is known to be of good quality and inexpensive.

The people of Kanita should be proud.

Moreover, the Bonjusan mountain range forms the backbone of the Tsugaru Peninsula. Not only cypress, cedar, beech, *katsura*, and larch trees grow on the mountains. The Kanagi area in the western part of the peninsula is known to be rich with wild herbs. In the Kanita region, bracken, royal fern, ginseng, bamboo shoot, butterbur, thistle, and mushrooms are easily gathered from the foothills close to town. Kanita has paddy fields and crop fields, and is blessed with seafood and vegetables, wild game, and mushrooms from the mountain. The reader may think of a town like Kanita as a different world, a place of perfect contentment, but Kanita seen from Kanranzan shows signs of weariness. There's no vitality. Even now, I write with excessive praise of Kanita. Here is a criticism but not enough for the people of Kanita to thrash me. The people of Kanita are gentle.

Gentleness is a virtue, but the townsmen's lethargy makes the town melancholy and lonely to the traveler.

The many natural blessings may be bad for the energy of the town. Kanita is a docile and quiet place. The seawall at the mouth of the river seemed half-built and abandoned. The ground is leveled to build a house, but the house is started but not finished, and pumpkins grow in the vacant lot of red soil. I could not see all of this from Kanranzan, but there seemed to be many buildings abandoned while under construction. When I asked N, "Does it mean, old schemers hampering the vigorous drive of the town administration?" this young councilman forced a smile and said, "Come here. Come here." The business method of a descendant of samurai and the political talk of a man of letters should be discreet.

My questions about the administration of Kanita ended in the idiotic result of only a smile of pity from the expert town councilman. The story I immediately recalled was a story of a failure of Degas. By chance, the master painter Edgar Degas in France's art circles sat on the same couch as the powerful politician Georges Clemenceau in the corridor of some dance theater in Paris. Without reserve, Degas embarked on a lofty political conversation with the powerful politician.

Degas said with passion, "If I became the prime minister, I believe in the importance of that responsibility and would cut ties to all loves; choose a simple, frugal life like an ascetic; and rent a very small room in a five-story walk-up close to the government offices. The apartment would only have a table and a humble iron bed. After returning home from the office, I would settle unfinished business on that table until late at night. When attacked by sleepiness, I would roll into bed with my clothes and shoes on. When I woke the following morning, I'd jump right up and enjoy eggs and soup while standing. Then I'd sling my bag over my shoulder and head to the office. That would be my life, I have no doubt!"

Clemenceau did not say a word. He only glared with scorn as if utterly appalled and looked hard at the face of the master painter. Mr. Degas seemed to wilt under his gaze and looked embarrassed. No one knew about that story of failure. Fifteen years later, he disclosed this to Mr. Bellelli, the closest of his few friends. Fifteen years is a long time. It looks like hiding at all costs. The arrogant master painter remembers being looked at with unconscious contempt by the professional politician and seemed chilled to the marrow of his bones, and, in spite of himself, remembers the feelings of pity stirred in his heart. The political musings of an artist are the origin of the wound. Degas is a good model. I'm nothing more than a destitute writer and will only talk about the cherry blossoms on Kanranzan and the love of my friends in Tsugaru. That seems safe.

Strong westerly winds blew the previous day and rattled the doors and papered *shoji* sliding doors of N's house.

"Kanita is a windy town," I said tossing out my usual enlightened understanding. Today, Kanita enjoyed fine weather as if softly laughing at my absurd remarks the previous evening. There was no gentle breeze. The cherry blossoms of Kanranzan seemed to be at their peak and faintly blooming in silence. The description of full bloom misses the mark. I felt the flower petals were washed in snow and chiseled slightly open. I thought they may be a different type of flower. The blue flower of the poet Novalis was an indistinct flower that makes me wonder if he imagined this flower. We sat cross-legged under the cherry blossoms and spread out the multi-tiered food boxes. Of course, the food had been prepared by N's wife.

Crabs and clams filled a large bamboo basket. And there was beer. Almost looking uncouth, I shelled the clams, sucked on crab legs, and even ate food from the boxes. The food in the boxes included transparent eggs packed into a squid's torso, toasted with soy sauce, and cut into round slices. They were delicious.

The returned soldier T mentioned how hot he was, took off his jacket, stood up half-naked, and began doing military exercises. Wearing a headband, he used a hand towel to wipe his dark face that bore a slight resemblance to the Burmese Chief Bamoo. The party gathered that day seemed slightly different from each other in their degree of enthusiasm. They appeared to want to draw out recollections about some novel from me. I answered what was asked. I followed the usual rules of pilgrimages by Basho of "A question must be answered," unless it conflicted with another important rule. Do not present the flaws of others and display one's own merits.

Disparaging others and taking pride in oneself is vile. I have done that vile thing. Many poets of other schools sniped at Basho but never behaved disgracefully. They did not make their eyebrows jump up, mouths turn down, square their shoulders, or abuse other novelists as I, an uncouth man, have done. My behavior has been unpleasant and shameful. Asked about the work of a fifty-year-old author in Japan, I thoughtlessly answered, "Not so good."

Recently, the past work of that author somehow provoked feelings close to awe in readers in Tokyo. Strangely, some came to call him God. A confession of liking that author offered a glimpse of the odd tendency to demonstrate the loftiness of the hobby of the reader and does a disservice. This may trouble the author who may force a smile. However, I previously looked from afar at the bizarre force of that author. From the silly heart of the typical Tsugaru man, "He becomes greedy, and simply got stronger by the fortunes of war at the time." I cannot be excited and docilely followed that trend.

By this time, I had reread most of that author's works and found them good but did not particularly feel the loftiness of the hobby. Instead, I wondered if this author found strength in greed. The world he described alternated between the joys and sorrows of the greedy petty bourgeois. Sometimes the hero of the work honestly reflected on his way of life. However, that aspect is particularly old-fashioned. If this sort of reflection is disagreeable, doing nothing is better and is separated from literary inexperience. Instead, it felt like being mired in stinginess. Strangely, many places appeared to be attempts at humor. Did he discard too much of himself? The reader does not docilely laugh because one trivial nerve is jittery. An immature criticism of the aristocracy was also heard but was ridiculous and a disservice. Can the aristocracy be thought of as untidy generosity?

During the French Revolution, the mob broke into the king's living quarters, but at that time, the French King Louis XVI went crazy, cackled with laughter, and snatched the revolutionary hat from the head of a rioter in the archery range and put it on his own head. Then he cried out "Vive la France!" The rioters hungry for blood were impressed by his perfect, mysterious dignity and joined the king in shouting "Vive la France!" Not one finger touched the king's body, and they obediently withdrew from the king's living quarters. A true aristocrat possessed this artless, unalterable dignity. The one who tightly closes his mouth and adjusts his collar often took the form of an aristocrat's servant. A pathetic word like aristocracy must not be used.

My companions drinking beer on Kanranzan in Kanita that day appeared to be ardent admirers of the fiftyish author and only questioned me about that author. Finally, I broke a rule of Basho and spoke abuse. I grew excited as I started to speak. As a result, my shoulders squared and my mouth drooped. The talk of aristocracy digressed at a strange place. The group did not express the least bit of agreement with my words. M, who came from Imabetsu, looking bewildered said, "We aren't saying aristocracy is stupid." He was embarrassed and looked like he was talking to himself. His words resembled careless remarks from a drunk. The others exchanged glances and smirked.

"In short," my voice seemed to shriek. Oh, I'm not criticizing a senior author. I got off track and said, "You can't be fooled by a man's appearance. King Louis XVI was a homely man rarely seen in history."

In the end, I was only further sidetracked.

"Well, I like his work," M declared his disagreement.

"Is that man's work good for Japan?" asked T from the Aomori hospital; he looked humble and conciliatory.

My position was wrong.

"That may be the best way. Well, it may be good. But while seated before me, isn't it horrible none of you have a word to say about my work?" I confessed my true motive with a smile.

Everyone smiled. I pushed my luck only to reveal my true intentions and said, "My work is a confused mess, but I have ambitions. I'm currently staggering under that heavy ambition. You probably see before you a filthy mess with sloppy ignorance, but I know true elegance. *Higashi* rice candies are shaped like pine needles, and daffodils are tossed into a celadon vase. I don't think they are elegant in any way. It's a hobby of the nouveau rich. And it's rude.

True elegance is a single white chrysanthemum on a massive black rock. It's no good if the foundation is not a large, dirty rock. That is true elegance. Young fellows like you consider the lyricism of a schoolgirl like a carnation supported by wire tossed in a cup to be artistic elegance."

My language offended. "I must not present the flaws of others and display my merits. Disparaging others and taking pride in oneself is vile." This pilgrimage rule of the old man resembles a serious truth. In fact, this is terrible. I have this vile habit. Even in literary circles in Tokyo, I unnerve everyone and am kept away as a grimy fool.

"Well, there's nothing I can do," I said and placed both hands behind me and turned my face up, "My work is so bad, talking about it will change nothing. Your appreciation of one-tenth of my work would be fine. Because you have no appreciation of my work, I blurt out the wrong thing. Please appreciate it. One-twentieth would be good. You must appreciate it."

Everyone laughed hysterically. The laughter spared my feelings, too. S, the manager at Kanita Hospital, rose and, with the soothing charity peculiar to a sophisticated man, said, "Shall we have a change of venue?"

He said he would have lunch prepared for everyone at the E Inn, the biggest in Kanita. With a glance, I asked T if that was all right.

"Great. We will have an enjoyable meal," T said as he rose to put on his jacket, "We planned this from the beginning. S has set aside some high-quality sake rations, so from now on, we will enjoy them. We can't let N be the only one treating us."

I obediently followed T's words. I felt reassured with T by my side.

The E Inn was very pretty. The alcove in the room was decent, and the toilet was clean. Inns on the east coast of the Tsugaru Peninsula are first-rate compared to those on the west coast. This may reflect their tradition from long ago of welcoming travelers from other provinces. In the past, when crossing to Hokkaido, boats always departed from Minmaya. This Sotogahama Road moves travelers from the entire country. Crabs were added to the trays of the inn. Anyone would say, "Of course, you're in Kanita." [Kanita is written using the kanji characters for *crabs* and *rice paddies*.]

T can't drink sake and ate his meal alone. Everyone else drank S's premium sake and put off eating. As he got drunk, S became cheerful.

"You see, I like novels by anyone all the same. When I read them, they're all interesting. Somehow, they're quite good. So I can't help but like novelists. I like any novelist so much I can't stand it. My son, he's three. I think he'll become a novelist. I even named him Fumio and write his name using the characters for *literature* and *man*. He's smart like you. Excuse me for saying, but your head is shaped like an open fan."

That's the first time I've heard my head looks broken. I should be well aware of every one of the various flaws in my looks, but I didn't realize the shape of my head was odd. Am I oblivious to many other defects? Immediately after I criticized other authors, I got very anxious. S cheerfully said, "Well, soon all the sake will be gone. Everyone is invited to my home. Well? It's okay. Come and meet my wife and Fumio. Please. If it's apple cider, we have more than enough in Kanita. Come to my home and have some. Okay."

He tempted me nonstop.

I was grateful for the temptation but was shattered about the crown of my head and wanted to return to N's home and go to bed. I was distressed by the thought of going to S's home and the inside of my head being seen through someplace on my skull which would lead to my being reviled. As usual, I gauged T's feelings. If T said to go, I was prepared to go. T looked serious while thinking.

"Should we go? S will get pretty drunk today, but he has been waiting a long time to enjoy your company."

I went. I stopped being sensitive about my skull. Thinking about it again, it was S's attempt at humor. I don't have much confidence in my appearance but must not fret about these trivialities. Not only my looks, my biggest flaw may now be my confidence.

We went to S's home and received an enthusiastic welcome that is the nature of the people of Tsugaru. This was a little confusing for me, despite being a native of Tsugaru. S stepped into his home and the rapid-fire orders for his wife began.

"Hey, I brought the guest from Tokyo home. He finally came. He's the Dazai fellow. Can you come here and greet him? Hurry, come and see him. And bring the sake. No, we already drank sake. Bring apple cider. Just one bottle. No, that's too little! Go and buy two more bottles. Wait.

"You're ripping up the dried cuttlefish hanging on the veranda. Wait. If you don't pound it first to tenderize, the ripping is no good. Wait. Don't hold it that way, I'll do it. This is how you pound dried cuttlefish. Like this. Ouch! This way. Hey, bring some soy sauce. It's no good without soy sauce. Get a cup. No, we need two. Hurry up. Wait. Are these teacups okay? Let's have a toast. Hey, go buy two more bottles. Wait. Go get the kid. It'll get him used to novelists. Let Dazai see him.

"How about the shape of this head? It looks like a busted bowl, kind of like yours. Great! Hey, go get the boy. Don't be so noisy. Isn't it rude to show this dirty kid to a guest? The bad taste of the newly rich. Quick, two more bottles of cider. It's no good if the guest runs away. Wait, you have to serve. Serve drinks to everybody. Go buy some cider from the lady next door. She wants sugar, give her a little.

"Wait, you can't give Auntie the sugar. I'm giving a gift of all the sugar in this house to our guest from Tokyo. Okay, don't forget. Give him all of it. And wrap it in newspaper and oiled paper then tie it up with string. The kid's gotta stop crying. Isn't that rude? The vulgarity of the nouveau rich. Aristocrats aren't like that. Get the sugar when the guests leave.

"Music. Music. Play a record. Maybe Schubert, Chopin, or Bach would be good. Play the music. Wait. What? That's Bach? Stop. It's too loud, we can't talk. Put on a quieter record. Wait. There's nothing to eat. Fry up some angler fish. Bring some of our delicious sauce. Will our guest like it? Wait. Serve the fried angler and *kayaki* fish stew with egg miso. You can't eat this anywhere but Tsugaru. There. Egg miso. The only egg miso. This is egg miso. This right here."

Nothing in this description is an exaggeration. A welcome resembling gales and angry waves is an expression of love by a Tsugaru native. Dried cuttlefish is a large cuttlefish that has been exposed to snowstorms, frozen, and dried. Its taste is light and refined and was enjoyed by Basho. Five or six fish hung from the eaves on the side of S's house. A wobbly S stood up and pulled off a few. He haphazardly pummeled them and his left thumb with a hammer. He poured a round of apple cider to everyone while twisting and squirming.

I realized the incident of the crown of my head was an attempt by S to make fun of me or an attempt at humor. S may earnestly respect my broad head. He may think it's a good thing. The simple honesty of Tsugaru's natives must be seen. He ended up repeatedly calling for egg miso, but this kayaki stew with egg miso probably warrants an explanation for the ordinary reader. Tsugaru has sukiyaki and chicken stew that are called beef kayaki and chicken kayaki. These are probably thought of as *kaiyaki*, the word for baked shellfish in the local dialect. Although that may not be so today, when I was young, large scallop shells were used for steaming meat in Tsugaru.

There may be the blind belief that varieties of broth come from the shells, which may have been believed in the old traditions of the aboriginal Ainu people. All of us grew up eating kayaki. For egg miso kayaki, a primitive dish, a shell is used as the pot for seafood and vegetables, shavings of dried bonito are added for flavor and everything is steamed, and then a hen's egg is dropped in before eating. When you're ill and have lost your appetite, this egg miso kayaki is made into a porridge and eaten. This was a dish unique to Tsugaru. S held this belief as he repeatedly called for me to eat it.

I asked to say goodbye to his wife who had been so hospitable and left S's home. I'd like the reader to pay particular attention to this. The welcome by S on that day expressed the love of a man of Tsugaru, moreover, a true-born native of Tsugaru. I can say without reservation that I often act exactly like S. When a friend comes from afar, I have no idea what to do. I've had the experience of my heart excitedly fluttering in meaningless confusion, and my head hitting the electric light breaking the bulb.

When an unexpected guest drops by during a meal, I immediately abandon my chopsticks and go out to the entryway while munching away and frown at the guest. I'm unable to put on the performance of making him wait while I calmly continue my meal. In essence, like S, I am distraught and puzzle over what to do. And if I bring out everything in the house as a treat, my guest is thrown off balance. Later, I apologize to the guest for my rudeness.

The expression of love by flinging away hesitation, hurling away neglect, grabbing them and throwing them away, and going as far as throwing away one's life may be thought of as rude violence to the people of the Kanto and Kansai regions so they stay away. On the way home, I felt like my fate was known by S, but he did not sympathize as I remembered from long ago. The expression of love by a Tsugaru native, if not given in a dose diluted by a little water, may be unreasonable to the people of other provinces. The people of Tokyo will simply put on airs and bring out a few scraps of food. Although they're not unsalted oyster mushrooms, because an excessive love is exposed, I, like Lord Kiso, may have been held in contempt by the arrogant, elegant people of Tokyo.

He urged me with, "Please help yourself. Please."

Later I heard that for the next week, S was embarrassed when he recalled the egg miso on that day and could not be around others without drinking sake. He usually appeared to be more sensitive than the others. This was also a trait of a native of Tsugaru. Normally, a true-born Tsugaru native is never a brutal savage. In contrast to the rash man from the city, he possesses immense grace and subtle sympathy.

Depending on the situation, when that restraint bursts open like a dam, he doesn't know what to do.

"The unsalted oysters are here at last."

He was mortified feeling that his urgency was frowned on by the frivolous man from the city. The following day, S became timid, drank sake, and went to visit a friend.

3

SOTOGAHAMA

I left S's home and went to N's. I drank more beer with N. That evening, T dropped by and stayed the night. The three of us slept in the back room. Early the next morning while I was still sleeping, T returned to Aomori by bus because he was busy at work.

"He was coughing," I said.

T woke up and coughed lightly as he dressed. While sleeping, my sharp ears heard a strange sadness. When I woke up, I immediately told N. When he got up and was putting on his pants, he said with a solemn look, "Yes, he was coughing." Whether drinking sake or not, he always looked somber. No, not only his face, his spirit was always stern.

"It wasn't a good cough," N also said. Although he seemed to be asleep, he clearly heard the coughs.

"It's willpower," said N in a defeated tone and buttoned his pants.

"None of us are well, are we?"

For a long time, both N and I have been fighting respiratory diseases. N has a bad case of asthma but seems to have fully recovered.

Before setting out on this trip, I promised to send a short story to a magazine published for the troops in Manchuria, and its deadline loomed. For that day and the next, I borrowed an inner room and worked. During that time, N was working in the rice polishing factory in another building. On the evening of the second day, N came to the room where I was working and asked, "Did you finish? Did you write two or three pages? I'll be done in about an hour. A week's worth of work done in two days. If you'd like, we could go out later. Work efficiency will improve. At least a little. It'll give you that final spurt of energy."

He promptly returned to the factory. Before ten minutes passed, he was back in my room.

"Are you finished? I have a little more to do. The machinery sounds good now. You haven't seen our factory, have you? It's dirty. It may be better if you don't see it. Well, I'll get back to work. And I'll sleep in the factory," he said and went back. Insensitive me finally realized N wanted me to see him energetically working in the factory. My dilemma was to finish my work soon and go to see him before he finished. I realized this and smiled. I quickly put my work in order and crossed the road and went to the rice-polishing factory in the other building. N was wearing a patched up and darned corduroy jacket and standing with both hands behind his back and a meaningful look on his face beside a huge rice-polishing machine with whirling rotations.

"That's lively," I shouted.

N spun around, happily smiled, and said, "Did you finish? Good. I have a little more to do. Come here. You can keep your sandals on."

I'm not so insensitive as to enter a rice-polishing factory wearing geta clogs. N had changed to a clean pair of straw *zori* sandals. I looked around but didn't see any indoor slippers. I just stood and smiled at the factory door. I wondered if I could go in barefoot but thought that overly hypocritical act would make N feel regret so I didn't go in barefoot. I have the very bad habit of performing commonsense good deeds.

"Now that's a big machine. You operate it all by yourself," I said with no flattery. Like me, N did not have many friends with technical knowledge.

"Oh, it's simple. When you turn these switches," as he was speaking, he turned switches here and there to show the motor coming to a dead stop, and easily operated the gigantic machine to display an avalanche of rice hulls and polished rice cascade down like a waterfall.

I caught sight of a small poster stuck to a pillar in the center of the factory. A man with a face shaped like a sake bottle was sitting cross-legged with his sleeves rolled up, and was holding a large cup at an angle. A house or a storehouse was inside the cup. Printed on this strange picture was a complaint, "Sake drinks you and drinks your home." I stared at this poster for a long time. N noticed and grinned while looking at my face. I grinned too. Both of us were guilty of this offense. It had the feeling of "Oh well, what can you do?" I sympathized with N who stuck that poster onto a post in his factory. Who holds a grudge against heavy drinkers? In my case, the twenty or so books I've written also decorate that large cup. I have no home or storehouse to drink. It should probably say "Sake drinks you and drinks your books."

Inside the factory, two large machines were not running. When I asked N what they did, he lightly sighed and said, "Oh, one machine makes rope and the other, straw mats. They're too hard to operate and too unruly for me. Four or five years ago, crops failed all around here, and orders for rice polishing dried up. It was bad. Everyday, I sat beside the furnace and smoked cigarettes. After a great deal of thinking, I bought these machines and plopped them in this corner of the factory. But I'm all thumbs and never got them running well. I was alone. My family of six had a meager existence. I didn't know what to do at that time."

In addition to his four-year-old son, N was raising the three children of his late younger sister. His sister's husband died in the war in northern China. Of course, N and his wife took in the three orphans and loved them like their own children. His wife told me N tends to spoil them too much. Of the three orphans, the oldest son is attending a technical school in Aomori. Every Saturday, he rides the bus seventeen miles from Aomori, walks the rest of the way home to Kanita, and gets home around midnight. "Uncle, Uncle," he calls out as he knocks on the door at the entryway.

N leaps from his bed to open the door and feverishly hugs the boy's shoulders. He only asks, "You walked the whole way? You walked?" His wife scolds him haphazardly and issues a quick succession of orders. "Here, have him drink some sugared hot water. Toast a rice cake, and warm up the noodles." While his wife remarks on how tired the child must be, "What?! What?" he says while waving his fist at her. During this quirky fight, their nephew explodes into laughter as does N while waving his fist, and his wife joins in. The matter is confused and remains unsettled. I felt this anecdote reveals a part of N's personality.

"Well, life has its ups and downs. Life goes on," I said. Thinking about my fate, too, I was touched. I envisioned the lonely figure of this good-natured friend alone in a corner of the factory weaving straw mats using an unfamiliar technique. I love this friend.

When we finished our respective work that night, we drank beer and talked about the crop failures in our province. N was a member of the Aomori Prefecture Local History Study Group and had quite a few documents about the history of this prefecture.

"Here's what has happened," said N and opened a book to show me. The following pages list an ominous table entitled *The Chronological Table of Crop Failures in Aomori*.

Genna year 1 Severe failure
Genna year 2 Severe failure
Kan'ei year 17 Severe failure
Kan'ei year 18 Severe failure
Kan'ei year 19 Minor failure
Meireki year 2 Minor failure
Kanbun year 6 Minor failure
Kanbun year 11 Minor failure
Enpo year 2 Minor failure
Enpo year 3 Minor failure
Enpo year 7 Minor failure
Tenwa year 1 Severe failure
Jokyo year 1 Minor failure
Genroku year 5 Severe failure
Genroku year 7 Severe failure
Genroku year 8 Severe failure
Genroku year 9 Minor failure
Genroku year 15 Moderate failure
Hoei year 2 Minor failure
Hoei year 3 Minor failure
Hoei year 4 Severe failure
Kyoho year 1 Minor failure

Kyoho year 5 Minor failure
Genbun year 2 Minor failure
Genbun year 5 Minor failure
Enkyo year 2 Severe failure
Enkyo year 4 Minor failure
Kan'en year 2 Severe failure
Horeki year 5 Severe failure
Meiwa year 4 Minor failure
An'ei year 5 Moderate failure
Tenmei year 2 Severe failure
Tenmei year 3 Severe failure
Tenmei year 6 Severe failure
Tenmei year 7 Moderate failure
Kansei year 1 Minor failure
Kansei year 5 Minor failure
Kansei year 11 Minor failure
Bunka year 10 Minor failure
Tenpo year 3 Moderate failure
Tenpo year 4 Severe failure
Tenpo year 6 Severe failure
Tenpo year 7 Severe failure
Tenpo year 8 Minor failure
Tenpo year 9 Severe failure
Tenpo year 10 Minor failure
Keio year 2 Minor failure
Meiji year 2 Minor failure
Meiji year 6 Minor failure
Meiji year 22 Minor failure
Meiji year 24 Minor failure
Meiji year 30 Minor failure
Meiji year 35 Severe failure
Meiji year 38 Severe failure
Taisho year 2 Minor failure
Showa year 6 Minor failure

Showa year 9 Minor failure
Showa year 10 Minor failure
Showa year 15 Moderate failure

THIS CHRONOLOGY WOULD GIVE anyone pause even if they were not from Tsugaru. Over the three hundred and thirty years from the first year of the Genna era, the summer campaign in the Siege of Osaka and the downfall of the Toyotomi until today, there have been about sixty crop failures. That comes to a crop failure every five years. Then N opened another book to show me. It said:

> The following year, Tenpo year 4, easterly winds blew in beginning on the auspicious first day of spring until the Girls' Day festival in March, but the accumulated snow had not disappeared and sleds were used by the farmers. At the height of May, the seedlings grew a little in clusters and should have blossomed in stages by that time of year, and planting finally began under these conditions.
>
> However, easterly winds blew violently over several days. After the hottest days of June came, billowy, dense clouds and fine, clear days were rarely seen...the cold grew every day and quilted clothes were worn again. Evenings were particularly cold. Even by the time of the nighttime Nebuta festival in July, no mosquitoes were heard on the roads. Few of them were heard inside the houses, and the use of mosquito nets was rare like the voices of locusts. (Author's note: Around the time of the seventh day of the seventh month of the lunar calendar, the brilliantly colored, giant lanterns in the forms of warriors or the rivalrous dragon and tiger are loaded onto carts and pulled. Young people dressed in costumes dance and parade down the streets in one of Tsugaru's annual events. The giant lanterns from different towns

always bump into each other, and fights break out. Large lanterns with the themes of Sakanoue no Tamuramaro and the Conquest of Emishi are paraded. One story says the Emishi people in the mountains were lured out and annihilated, but the story has little credence. Not only Tsugaru, similar customs are found in other parts of Tohoku. Would it be a mistake to think of floats for summer festivals in Tohoku?)

The hot weather began around July 6, and people wore unlined kimonos before the Bon Festival. The popular dances of the Bon Festival livened up around the thirteenth when the ears have appeared on most of the grains of early-ripening rice. Around the fifteenth and the sixteenth, a band of bright, white sunlight resembled a mirror at night. At midnight on the seventeenth, the dancers scattered and the crowds on the streets thinned. With the gradual arrival of dawn, an unexpected heavy frost settled on and bent the necks of the early-ripening rice. The old and young still out on the streets saw this and shed many tears.

More than miserable, an indescribable situation is described. When we were very young, the old people told us about the horrendous circumstance of the *kegazu*. (In Tsugaru, kegazu means crop failure. It may be dialect for starvation.) Although young, I became despondent and was close to tears. Returning to my home province after a long time and being plainly shown this sort of record, my feelings passed through sorrow and turned to an impossible-to-understand rage.

"This is awful," I said, "The scientific world makes all kinds of extravagant claims but can't teach farmers how to prevent these crop failures. That's irresponsible."

"No, experts are engaged in a myriad of research. Varieties of rice resistant to damage by cold weather are being improved. Various tactics are also devised for the planting period. Although the total crop failures of the past are gone, once every four or five years, the indefensible happens."

"It's ridiculous," I said not angry at anyone in particular and cursed.

N smiled and said, "People also live in the desert. The only choice is to get angry. Peculiar human feelings are born from this kind of climate, too."

"These are not excessively nice human feelings. There are no places with balmy spring weather, and I'm always losing ground to artists in the southern provinces."

"But you aren't losing, are you? From long ago, the Tsugaru region was never attacked and destroyed by people from other provinces. Although beaten, they were not defeated. Isn't the Eighth Division a national treasure?"

The blood of our ancestors haunted by crop failures from birth and raised by sipping rain and dew is transmitted to us. The virtue of balmy spring weather is enviable, without a doubt, but I can do nothing other than work as hard as possible to make splendid flowers bloom in the sorrowful blood of the ancestors. Without lamenting past sorrows in vain, it may be better to take enormous pride in the tradition of struggling through hardship like N does. Moreover, Tsugaru no longer endlessly repeats the disastrous picture of hell.

The following day, N told me how to travel north by bus along the Sotogahama Road. I stayed a night in Minmaya and then walked a lonely road along the coastline to Cape Tappi at the northern tip of Honshu. Even in the desolate and forlorn hamlets between Minmaya and Tappi, the homes are reinforced against gales and unflinching against the angry waves. The excellent health of the people of Tsugaru is lovingly displayed. A serene life unfolded before my eyes in the bright atmosphere of the elegant seaports reaching Minmaya and each hamlet south of it, particularly Minmaya and Imabetsu. Oh, there's no point in fearing the shadow of kegazu.

Below is an enjoyable composition written by Professor Sato Hiroshi. I'll borrow his writings as a merry farewell toast from the people of Tsugaru to erase the melancholy of the reader of my writings. In an outline of industry in Oshu, Professor Sato writes:

> Oshu is the territory of the Emishi people who hide in the grass when attacked and enter the mountains when followed. In Oshu, natural barriers are formed by mountains rising above other mountains and hinder passage. Oshu is enclosed by the Sea of Japan with its rough waves and unsuitable for shipping by sea and the Pacific Ocean with many serrated capes and bays cut off by the northern mountain range and unreachable. Snowstorms often assault Oshu in the winter, the coldest part of Honshu. During ancient times, Oshu suffered dozens of crop failures. In contrast to forty percent of Kyushu being arable land, Oshu has a pitiful fifteen percent. From any perspective, Oshu is controlled by unfortunate natural conditions but today supports a population of 6.3 million and could form the base for any industry.

Reading any geography book will tell you the clothes, food, and dwellings are simple when living in the far away lands of Oshu and the northeastern part of Honshu. They are satisfied living under thatched roofing, shingled roofing, cedar bark roofing from the old days, and tin roofs today, wear wrapping cloths on their heads, *monpe* work pants, and eat average or worse than average, plain foods. What is authentic? Is the land of

Oshu blessed with industry? Will twentieth-century culture that takes pride in speed not reach only the Tohoku region? No, that is already the Oshu of the past. If people wish to talk about present-day Oshu, the repressed emerging power appeared in Italy right before the Renaissance must be recognized in this land of Oshu. The emperor's spirit related to the education of the Meiji Emperor about culture and industry swiftly permeated the entire country of Oshu. This encouraged the decline of the unpleasant nasal sounds peculiar to the people of Oshu and the advance of standard language. The glory of enlightenment was given to the uneducated households that had fallen into a primitive state. From today's perspective, development and cultivation are increasing well-fertilized fields bearing products every moment. With added improvements, cattle farming, forestry, and fisheries will grow prosperous day by day. And given the sparse distribution of inhabitants, this land has plenty of room for future development.

During the era of expansion, the Yamato people, the ethnic Japanese, moved north from each region and reached Oshu like large flocks of migratory birds of starlings, ducks, chickadees, and geese roaming this region in search of food, and conquered the Ezo, the non-Yamato people. They hunted in the mountains, fished in the rivers, were attracted by various natural resources, and wandered all over. Thus, after several generations passed, the people living here are a part of the land in their own way. They grew rice on the plains of Akita, Shonai, and Tsugaru, planted trees in the mountains of Kitaoku, grazed horses on the plains, and were dedicated to the fisheries near the sea. These provided the foundations of today's thriving industries.

The six provinces of Oshu and the 6.3 million

inhabitants do not neglect the industries developed by their predecessors and develop them further. Migratory birds wander for eternity. The simple people of Tohoku no longer wander but grow rice, sell apples, and let splendid foals with fine hair run through the expansive green plains lined by beautiful luxuriant forests. And fishing boats loaded with dancing silvery fish enter the harbors.

There was no spontaneous running up for a polite handshake to express appreciation. The next day, I traveled north to Sotogahama in Oshu accompanied by N. Before setting out, the first problem was sake.

"Would you like some sake? Can a couple of bottles of beer fit in your backpack?" his wife asked. I felt ashamed. I wondered if I was born a man into the disgraceful race of heavy drinkers.

"Oh no, I'm fine. If there's none, it's fine," I said vaguely stumbling over my words while picking up my backpack and hurried out of the house, almost running away.

N followed me out. I honestly said to him, "Sorry. I feel a chill when I hear sake. It's a straw mat of needles."

He appeared to have the same thought and blushed as he chuckled.

"I don't have the strength by myself. When I see your face, I have to drink. M in Imabetsu gathered sake rations a little at a time from his neighborhood, so why not stop at Imabetsu?"

I released a complicated sigh and said, "It'll put everyone to too much trouble."

Our plan was to first go straight to Tappi from Kanita and return by walking and by bus. However, strong easterly winds began in the morning. The weather could be described as rough. The ferry we planned to board was canceled. Our plans changed and we went by bus. The bus was unusually empty, and the two of us could stretch out in our seats. After going north for about an hour along the Sotogahama Road, the winds gradually subsided and blue skies peeked out. With weather in this state, I believed the ferry probably would not depart.

If we dropped by M's house in Imabetsu and the boat was running, we would have a drink and return by boat from the port at Imabetsu. I thought that going the same route by land both ways was smart and of no consequence. From the bus, N pointed out and explained various landmarks. We were approaching a fortified zone, and I probably should have been discreetly writing down N's kind descriptions.

Few Ezo dwellings from long ago were seen in this area. Was the weather clearing up? Which villages were visible? The travel diary *Toyuki* (Journey to the East) of the famous doctor Tachibana Nankei published during the Kansei era states:

> Since the beginning of heaven and earth, times have never been as peaceful as now. From the Kikai and Yakyu islands in the west to Sotogahama in Oshu in the east, laws must be scrupulously obeyed. During ancient times, the island of Yakyu sounded like the foreign country of Yakyu. Oshu was partly inhabited by the Ezo people and was seen as the home of foreigners until recently. There are many different names for the place names in the southern region and in Tsugaru. The villages along the Sotogahama Road have names like Tappi, Horozuki, Uchimappe, Sotomappe, Imabetsu, and Utetsu.
>
> These are all Ezo words. Even today in areas like

Utetsu, there are customs and Tsugaru natives who are related to the Ezo people, but they have come to disdain being called Ezo. Not only the Utetsu area, the villagers in the southern part and in Tsugaru are probably Ezo. In some places, these people rapidly changed their customs and language as they came under imperial rule and have become more like the Japanese than their ancestors. For this reason, manners and refined civilization, understandably, may still need to advance.

These words were written one hundred and fifty years ago. If Dr. Nankei now underground could ride a bus today on level concrete roads, he would be dazed and snapping his head all around to see, or he may lament as in *Kozo no Yuki Imaizuko* (Where are the snows of yesteryear).

Nankei's *Toyuki* and *Saiyuki* (Journey to the West) are counted among the masterpieces of the Edo era. The legend notes read like a confession:

If I travel for medical knowledge, although I will chat about medical matters, I will record them elsewhere and show them to like-minded people. Although these writings record my observations during my travels, I have not verified the facts of these observations, and there are probably many errors.

It's fine to say an article resembling nonsense achieves little but is adequate to stimulate the reader's curiosity. I will not mention other regions and limit my examples to articles about the Sotogahama region. Without raising doubts, he also writes:

Minmaya, Oshu includes the port for the Matsumae sea crossing, Sotogahama in the Tsugaru domain, and

Tohoku in Japan. Long ago, Minamoto no Yoshitsune escaped the Takadachi fortress and came here to cross over to Ezo (now Hokkaido). Unfavorable winds for a crossing delayed him for a few days. Unable to bear it, he placed his Kannon statue on a rock on the seafloor and prayed for favorable winds. The winds shifted immediately, and he safely crossed to Matsumae. Today, this statue is kept at a local shrine and is known as the Kannon of Yoshitsune's Wind Prayer. A large rock at the water's edge was pierced by three holes in a line like in a stable. That was the place where Yoshitsune's horses were hitched. This is the origin of the name of Minmaya (three horses stable) for this place.

He continues.

There is a place called Tairadate in Sotogahama in Tsugaru, Oshu. A place jutting into the Iwaoishi Sea north of here is called Ishizaki. A short time after passing over Ishizaki is Shudani. Narrow mountain streams flow from the towering mountains and drop into the sea. All the soil and rocks in this valley are colored vermilion. I feel awakened by the water that turned red and the brilliant colors of the morning sun reflected by the wet rocks. Many of the pebbles at this place dropping into the sea are vermilion. They say all the fish in the northern sea are red. From the impressions of redness of places in the valley, both the sentient and the non-sentient mysteriously emit the color red from the fish in the sea and even in the rocks.

I think I'll stop here.

He frightens you with his writing about a strange fish called the *Old Man* living in the northern seas.

No human has seen the entire body of this huge fish that stretches five to seven miles long. In rare sightings, it resembles several large islands floating on the ocean. Little by little the tail fin on the back of this Old Man becomes visible. It swallows a whale twenty or thirty fathoms down like a whale swallows sardines. Therefore, when this fish comes, the whales flee to the east and west....

When delayed one night in Minmaya, the elderly folks from nearby homes came to visit; the grandfathers and grandmothers gathered around the hearth in the home. Together they talked about various subjects. No story was as chilling as the tsunami at Matsumae twenty or thirty years ago. At that time, the winds were quiet and the rains were far away, but they felt empty. At moments during the night, shooting stars flew across the empty sky to the east and to the west and gradually grew to a large number. Four or five days earlier, all sorts of deities flew through the sky even in broad daylight. They looked like court officials in full dress riding horseback or riding dragons or riding clouds or riding a type of rhinoceros or elephant, and transformed into a white costume. With the appearance of red and blue colors, the forms became large and small and fill the skies with strange-looking deities and Buddhas flying to the east and to the west.

Every day, we all went outside and prayed in gratitude. For four or five days, we prayed and talked about the extraordinary events before our eyes. One evening, while looking out to sea, far off in the distance we saw something like a mountain of pure white snow. Look at that! As we looked at the mysterious object in the sea, it slowly crept toward us. Looking closely, above what appeared to be the island mountain, we saw a gigantic wave coming towards us. Tsunami! Run! Young and old, men and women scrambled to get away, but it approached rapidly. Of the houses, fields, plants, and birds and animals, not even a few remained. Only waste remained on the sea floor. Not one person from the villages on the coast survived. For that reason, the deities flying in the clouds at the beginning foretold this horrible event and were urging us to flee this land.

Events that seemed sacrilegious or from a dream are fluently written in plain text. In the current environment, I thought it best not to be too specific. You may call this absurd, but it's fun to copy the travel diary of an ancient and be immersed in a world resembling a fairy tale. In fact, I had reasons for including a few excerpts from the articles in *Toyuki*. I have one more. I'd like to introduce an article I think will especially amuse aficionados of novels.

Around the time I was in Sotogahama in Tsugaru, Oshu, a local government official repeatedly asked if anyone was from Tango. When asked why, his reason was a god of Mount Iwaki in Tsugaru detests men from Tango. If anyone from Tango sneaks into this land, the gods wreak havoc with the weather. The wind and rain never cease, and ships cannot enter or leave causing great hardship to the Tsugaru region.

Terrible winds continued while I was there prompting me to search for someone from Tango. Any time the weather deteriorated, the officials conducted strict inquiries. If one had entered, he was quickly expelled. When anyone from Tango left the domain of Tsugaru, the weather immediately cleared up and the winds calmed down. As well as being a hatred handed down as a custom, curiously, the officials conducted searches each time.

At Aomori, Minmaya, and other ports along the Sotogahama Road, the people of Tango were the most hated. When questioned closely for the reason why they were hated so much, the story was the god of Mount Iwaki in this province enshrines Princess Anju in the land of her birth.

The princess wandered into the province of Tango and was tormented by the bailiff Sansho. These days, anyone from that province is hated; winds and rain start; and the gods of Iwaki go wild. Along the 220 miles of Sotogahama, most of the people fished and hunted for a living or worked in ship transportation, and always prayed for favorable winds. However, whenever the weather deteriorated, the people of Tango were hated. This opinion is held at the borders, the southern part of Matsumae, and the ports, and hatred is sent to people from Tango. This much malice runs deep in people.

This story is strange. The people of Tango are greatly inconvenienced. The land of Tango is north of Kyoto Prefecture, but people from there who come to Tsugaru must pay dearly. We learned of the story of Princess Anju and Prince Tsushi as children from picture books. *Sansho Dayu* (Sansho the Bailiff), the masterpiece written by Mori Ogai, is well known to anyone who loves novels. The beautiful sister and brother in this tragic tale were born in Tsugaru and enshrined in Mount Iwaki after their deaths. This is not well known. In fact, I find the story doubtful.

Nankei calmly wrote about Yoshitsune coming to Tsugaru, the seven-mile-long fish, the red scales of fish and the red water dyed by the color of dissolved rocks. These may be irresponsible articles following the customary ritual of not verifying the facts. Understandably, the story of Princess Anju and Prince Tsushi also appeared in the article *Iwaki-san Gongen* (Buddha Incarnations on Mount Iwaki) in the Chinese-Japanese encyclopedia *Sancai Tuhui* (Illustrations of the Three Powers). This encyclopedia has a little Chinese writing and is hard to read, but I'm confident in writing, "In a story passed down, long ago, a man named Iwaki Hangan Masauji was lord of this province (Tsugaru). In the winter of the first year of the Eiho era (1081) while living in Kyoto, he was deported to Saikai after being slandered by some unknown person. He had two children in the province, a daughter named Anju and her younger brother named Tsushiomaru. They wandered with their mother, passed through Dewa, and reached Echigo. At Naoe Bay..." When the end is reached, the speech dissolves into, "I have doubts they are enshrined in Mount Iwaki in Tsugaru that is over two hundred miles to the north of Iwaki."

In *Sansho the Bailiff*, Ogai writes "...leaves the house in Shinobu-gun, Iwashiro." In other words, the characters for the name Iwaki are read as *Iwaki* and as *Iwashiro*. I believe confusion set in and eventually that legend was adopted by Mount Iwaki in Tsugaru. But the people in Tsugaru long ago firmly believed Anju and Tsushio were children of Tsugaru and fittingly cursed Sansho the Bailiff. We as sympathizers of Anju and Tsushio were delighted with the belief that if anyone from Tango entered Tsugaru, the weather worsened.

I'll stop here with the folklore of Sotogahama. Our bus arrived in Imabetsu, where M lives, around noon. As I said earlier, Imabetsu is a port city that could be described as modern. Its population was close to four thousand. N led me to M's house for our visit. His wife greeted us and said he was out. It seems he was a little ill. Whenever I encounter this kind of situation at another's home, I have the habit of immediately wondering if I had a fight with him. Was I right or wrong? The appearance of an author or a newspaper reporter at a nice home easily makes people uneasy. As an author, that should pain me. An author who has not experienced this pain is stupid.

"Where did he go?" N casually asked. He set down his backpack and said, "I'll rest here for a while," and sat on a step at the entrance.

"I'll call him," she said.

"Oh, I'm sorry," said N calmly and asked, "Is he at the hospital?"

"Uh, I believe so," softly said the attractive, shy woman as she slipped on her geta clogs and went outside. M worked in a hospital in Imabetsu.

I sat down beside N on the step and we waited.

"Did he know we were coming?"

"Uh, well," said N and calmly smoked his cigarette.

"Unfortunately, you can't show up at lunchtime," I said a little worried.

"Well, we brought our own lunches," he said smugly. The last samurai Saigo Takamori was probably like this, too.

M returned home. He smiled bashfully and said, "Welcome."

"Sorry but we can't stay," said N and stood, "If we're going by boat, I'd like to go right away by boat to Tappi."

"Oh," said M and slightly bowed his head, "Well, I'll see if it's running."

M headed to the harbor to ask, but the boat was canceled.

"That settles it," said my guide not looking particularly disappointed, "Well, will you let us rest here to eat our bento lunch?"

"We're fine sitting here," I said with great reserve.

"Won't you come in?" M meekly asked.

"Why don't we go in?" said N and calmly removed his gaiters, "We'll plan the next step of our itinerary more carefully."

We passed into M's study. There was a small hearth, and a charcoal fire crackled. The bookshelves were stuffed with books. The collected works of Paul Valery and those of Izumi Kyoka were included. Nankei, who concluded with confidence "manners and refined civilization still need to advance," may come this far and faint.

"I have sake," said the genteel M and blushed, "Shall we have a drink?"

"No, no, if we drink here," N started to say but laughed it off.

"It's all right," said M, who grasped the situation immediately, "I set aside sake for you to take to Tappi."

"Ha, ha," said N and playfully added, "Oh no, but if we start drinking now, we may not be able to go to Tappi tomorrow."

M's wife silently brought in the bottle of sake. From the beginning, his wife was a quiet woman but was not particularly angry at us. I thought about it again favorably to me.

"Should we have a little but not enough to get drunk?" I proposed to N.

"If I drink, I'll get drunk," said N with authority, "Shall we stay in Minmaya tonight?"

"That's good. Today, you can spend a relaxed day in Imabetsu and walk to Minmaya. A leisurely walk would take about an hour, right? No matter how much you drink, the walk is a cinch," M suggested. We decided to spend the night in Minmaya and began drinking.

From the moment I entered this room, there was one obstacle. The collection of literary essays of the fifty-year-old writer I criticized in Kanita was neatly arranged on M's desk. Readers are great people. Although I abused this author so much on that day on Kanranzan in Kanita, M's trust in this author did not seem the least bit shaky.

"Hey, let me see this book."

I was worried and restless. I borrowed M's book, flipped it open, and began reading with keen eyes. I wanted to pick out any flaw and sing a victory song. However, the place I read seemed to have been written when the writer was on edge and thoroughly absorbed. I read in silence. I read one page, two pages, three pages, and finally five pages, then I tossed the book aside.

"The part I read was fairly good. But his other works have some bad parts," said the sore loser.

M seemed delighted.

"The binding is splendid," I quietly said and added sour grapes, "If a large type like this is printed on this sort of high-grade paper, the text will look magnificent."

M ignored me and did not say a word but smiled the smile of a winner. The truth is I did not feel humiliated. I was relieved the text I read was good. More than finding errors and singing a song of triumph, I didn't understand how good that feeling is. I'm not lying. I long to read fine compositions.

Hongaku-ji is a famous temple in Imabetsu. It is known that the head priest was the great priest Teiden. He was written about in *Aomori-ken Tsuushi* (A Brief History of Aomori Prefecture) by Takeuchi Umpei.

It states:

> Priest Teiden was the child of Niiyama Jinzaemon of Imabetsu and soon became a disciple in the Hirosaki Seigan-ji Temple and trained at Senshou-ji Temple in Iwakidaira for fifteen years. From the age of twenty-

nine, he served as the chief priest at Hongaku-ji Temple in Imabetsu, Tsugaru. For his education until Koho year 16 (1731) when he reached forty-two years of age, he traveled to neighboring provinces in addition to traveling throughout the Tsugaru region. As during a memorial service for the erection of the gilt bronze pagoda in Koho year 12, throngs of pious men and women from the territory, such as the southern region, Akita, and Matsumae, were seen on pilgrimage to the temple.

N, the Sotogahama guide and town councilor, suggested we visit that temple.

"Talking about literature is fine, but your talk is not general. Some of it is curious. So no matter how much time passes, you will never become famous. Now, Priest Teiden," said N, who was fairly drunk, "Priest Teiden delayed explaining Buddha's teachings and first planned to advance the welfare of the people. If he hadn't, the people wouldn't have listened to anything about Buddha's teachings, you see. Priest Teiden revived industry and..." he interrupted himself with a burst of laughter.

"Well, let's go. It would be a shame to come to Imabetsu and not see Hongaku-ji. Priest Teiden is the pride of Sotogahama. I say that but the truth is I still haven't seen it. This is a good opportunity. I want to see it today. Why don't we all go?"

As we drank, I talked about literature with so-called weird spots with M. He seemed to agree. But N's passion for Priest Teiden was intense, and he finally got our lazy butts up.

"Let's drop by this Hongaku-ji Temple then walk straight to Minmaya," I said as I sat on the step an the entryway and fastened my gaiters.

"Well, are you coming?" I invited M.

"Yes, I should go with you to Minmaya."

"I'd be grateful if you did. With this energy, I think we can have a long discussion about the town administration of Kanita at an inn in Minmaya. The truth is I've become melancholy. When I see you, I'm reassured. Mrs. M, tonight I'm borrowing your husband."

"All right," she said with a smile. She seemed more relaxed. No, she was probably resigned.

We filled water bottles with sake and set out in good cheer. Along the way, N shouted, "Priest Teiden! Priest Teiden!" The roof of the temple was in our sights when we came across an old woman selling fish. The cart she pulled was stacked with an assortment of fish. I found a sea bream about two feet long.

"How much for this sea bream?" I asked without guessing the price.

"One yen, seventy sen."

Cheap, I thought.

I bought it. However, after buying it, I was poor. And I was going to a temple. Carrying a two-feet-long fish to a temple was a strange plan. I became glum along the way.

"That purchase made no sense," said N twisting his mouth in scorn, "Why did you buy that?"

"You're wrong, we're going to an inn in Minmaya. I'll have them salt and grill it and serve it on a large plate for three people."

"Well, you're thinking is peculiar. I'd like to see what kind of marriage ceremony you had."

"Anyway, aren't you grateful I was able to soak up a bit of luxury for one yen seventy sen?"

"I'm not thankful. Around here one yen seventy sen is a lot. In fact, you aren't a skilled shopper."

"Really?" I said, disappointed.

I finally entered the temple grounds with the two-feet-long fish dangling down.

"What should I do?" I quietly conferred with M, "I'm at a loss."

"So that's it," said M looking pensive, "I'll go to the temple and get a newspaper or something. Wait here. I'll be right back."

M went to the back of the temple kitchen and returned with newspapers and string. He wrapped up the problem fish and put it in my backpack. I was relieved and looked up at the temple gate and did not see a particularly splendid building.

"It's not much of a temple, is it?" I whispered to N.

"No, no, no. Inside is much better. Let's go in and listen to the priest's explanation."

I felt depressed and plodded behind N. From then on, our experience would be bitter. The priest was out, but his fifty-year-old wife came out and gave us a tour of the main temple. A prolonged explanation followed. The whole time we sat in the proper kneeling position and listened. When she paused and happily stood, N drew closer and said, "If I may, I'd like to ask one more question. Around when did Priest Teiden build this temple?"

"What do you mean? Saint Teiden did not found this temple. Teiden was the fifth generation priest of this temple's founder and revived the sect," she said and continued her drawn-out explanation.

"So that's what happened," said N and blankly stared, "If I may, I have another question. This Priest Teizan…" He said Priest Teizan and was in a muddle.

An enthusiastic N kept inching closer, asking questions and getting answers, until he was separated by a gap the width of a sheet of paper from the knees of the old woman. It would be dark soon. My spirits sank thinking about having to leave for Minmaya.

"That wonderful, large tablet over there was written by Ono Kurobei."

"Is that so?" admired N, "And who is Ono Kurobei..."

"You've probably heard of him. He is one of the Loyal Retainers."

I think she said loyal retainer.

She said, "He died on this ground at the age of forty-seven and was a man of deep faith and often made huge donations to this temple."

At this moment, M rose and went over to stand before the old woman and held out an object wrapped in white paper from his inner pocket, and bowed without speaking a word. He turned to N and whispered, "We must say good-bye."

"Oh, yes, we must be going," said N with a generous heart and complimented the old woman, "Your talk was excellent," and finally stood to leave.

Later when I asked N if he recalled one thing told to him by the woman, he said no. We were amazed.

I said, "You fired off questions with so much passion."

"Oh, I wasn't paying the least bit of attention. I was terribly drunk. I thought you two wanted to learn more. I forced myself to keep speaking," he said, laying bare his empty sacrifice.

We arrived at the Minmaya inn after sunset and were escorted to a small, clean room on the second floor in the front. All the inns in Sotogahama were high class, unlike the town. We could see the sea from our room. Light showers began, and the white seas calmed.

"This isn't bad. We have the sea bream and can leisurely eat while gazing at the rain on the sea," I said while retrieving the wrapped fish from my backpack.

I handed the package to the housemaid and said, "This is sea bream. Please salt and grill it then bring it back."

The maid looked slow-witted and only said, "Yes." She seemed distracted when she took the package and left the room.

"Do you think she understood?" asked N who seemed to have the same concern. He called to stop her and to give further instructions but not clearly.

"Salt and grill this as is. There are three of us, but there's no need to cut it in three. Most importantly, three equal pieces are not needed. Do you understand?"

Of course, the maid replied with a casual, "Yes."

Finally, the meal arrived. The unsmiling, obtuse maid said, "The fish is salted and grilled, but we don't have sake today."

"Well, we'll have to drink the sake we brought with us."

"It seems so," said N and drew a water bottle closer, "Excuse me, please bring two sake bottles and three cups."

We were joking about three not being enough when the sea bream arrived. N's caution about no need to cut the fish into three pieces led to a foolish result. The head, the tail, and the bones were gone. Only the salted and grilled flesh of the fish cut into five pieces was placed on an inelegant, faded plate. I'm never particular about food. I didn't buy the two-feet-long sea bream because I wanted to eat it. Dear reader, you probably understand. I wanted the fish with the tail intact to be grilled and placed on a large plate as a vision for me to gaze at. The predicament was not whether to eat the fish or not. I wanted to enjoy the fine feeling of drinking sake while gazing at the fish. N's explanation to keep the fish intact was peculiar, but the callousness of the inn worker who decided to slice up the sea bream into five pieces was aggravating and despicable. I was provoked.

"No one asked for this."

I glared at the five pieces of grilled fish (no longer sea bream, just grilled fish) dumped on the plate, and I wanted to cry. Even if the fish had been prepared as sashimi, I still would have been disappointed. What happened to the head and the bones? Did they throw away the splendid, huge head? An inn in a land with an abundance of fish creates an unimaginative dish and knows nothing of cooking techniques.

"Don't get mad. It's good," said N with his well-rounded personality and selected a piece of grilled fish with chopsticks, "All right. You can eat all of it by yourself. Eat. I'm not eating. Can you gobble this up? As usual, I made a mistake. There was no need for three equal pieces. That idiot maid was confused by my extraneous comments in the pretentious words used in a budget meeting of the Kanita Town Council. I was wrong and am sorry."

N gave an easy laugh and said, "But isn't this amusing? I said not to cut into three pieces, so they cut it into five. The people here are smart. Elegant. Let's toast. A toast."

I was keen for a meaningless toast. Was it resentment over the sea bream? I got dead drunk, reached a vague agitation, and dropped off to sleep. Even now as I remember, I'm still upset over that sea bream. Usually, I'm insensitive.

I woke the next morning to rain. I went downstairs to ask about the boats, but the inn attendant said they were canceled for the day. We had no choice but to walk along the coast to Tappi and decided to leave when the rain cleared. We crawled back into our futons and chatted.

"Once upon a time, there were two sisters," I began a fairy tale, "The sisters were given the same number of pinecones by their mother and ordered to make rice and miso soup. The stingy and cautious younger sister carefully placed each pinecone in an oven and burned them up. She was unable to simmer a satisfactory miso soup or rice. The older sister had a gentle, carefree nature and dumped all her pinecones to feed the oven. With that fire, she made rice and, with the leftover charcoal, made the miso soup.

"Do you know that story? Let's have a drink. Isn't there one more bottle of the sake we were going to take to Tappi? Let's drink that. We can't be stingy. Drinking it all at once is no big deal. If we do, charcoal will be left over. No, it's all right even if nothing remains. When we go to Tappi, what will happen? Isn't it all right if there's no sake to drink in Tappi? No one will die. Falling asleep without drinking sake, and thinking about your past and future are not bad things."

"Okay, I get it," said N and sprung up, "Let's do everything like the older sister. Let's drink it all at once."

We gathered around the hearth and warmed the sake in the kettle. We waited for the rain to stop by drinking the rest of the sake.

Around noon, the rain stopped. We gulped down breakfast and prepared to leave. The cloudy day was a bit chilly. N and I parted from M at the front of the inn and headed north.

"Shall we climb up?"

N stopped in front of the shrine archway of the stone of Gikei-ji Temple. The name of Somebody Matsumae, the donor of the archway, was carved into a pillar.

"Okay."

We passed through the stone archway and climbed the stone steps. There were many steps to the top. Raindrops fell from the tops of the trees on both sides of the steps.

"Is this it?"

A timeworn Chinese-style temple stood at the peak of the small mountain cut with the stone stairs. The crest of

Sasarindou no Minamoto was affixed to the temple door. For some reason, I was struck with disgust and again asked, "Is this it?"

"It is," said N in a dopey voice.

Long ago, Minamoto no Yoshitsune escaped to Takadachi. When he couldn't cross over to Ezo, he came to this place. Without favorable winds to cross, he stayed for several days. Unable to bear the wait, he placed the statue of Kannon, the goddess of mercy, in his possession on a rock on the sea floor and prayed for favorable winds. The winds changed at once and he crossed safely to Matsumae. That statue is now in this temple and is called the Kannon of Yoshitsune's Wind Prayer.

This temple is usually introduced first in *Toyuki*.

We walked down the steps in silence.

"Look here and there on the stairs, are those depressions? Could they be the footprints of Benkei or the hoof prints of Yoshitsune's horse? What's the story?" asked N and had to laugh. I wanted to believe, but it was no good. There is a rock where you leave the archway. The reason is given in *Toyuki*:

> A large rock at the water's edge was pierced by three holes in a line like in a stable. That was the place for hitching Yoshitsune's horses. This is the origin of the name of Minmaya (three horses stable) for this place.

I said, "This says two young delinquents from the Kamakura era came to ask for shelter for one night. One was someone with something to hide, Kurou Hogan, the name given to Yoshitsune by the Imperial Court, and the other was a bearded man Musashibo Benkei, the warrior monk who served Yoshitsune. And surely they deceived a country girl along the way. Tsugaru has too many legends about Yoshitsune. Not only in the Kamakura era, Yoshitsune and Benkei may have been prowling around three hundred years later in the Edo era, too."

"But Benkei's role was probably drab," said N.

N's beard was thicker than mine and looked anxious he may be forced into Benkei's role.

"Was his role to lug heavy equipment?"

As we talked, we imagined and found delight in the wandering life of the two young delinquents and were moved by envy.

"There are a lot of pretty ladies around here," I whispered. The young women we glimpsed passing through the shadows of houses in the hamlets soon vanished. All were elegant with pale, white skin and a fresh appearance. Their hands and feet were probably soft.

"That's true. If you say so, that's true."

Few men are as indifferent to women as N. It's the sake.

"Now, you probably won't believe me when I tell you my name is Yoshitsune," I said imagining such stupidity.

We spoke this nonsense back and forth during our stroll but gradually quickened our pace into a full-fledged, two-man race. All talking stopped. We sobered up from our drunkenness brought on by the Minmaya sake. It was terribly cold. We had to hurry. Both of us looked solemn and strutted with determination. The sea breeze strengthened. I pull down the brim of my hat that almost blew off several times. Finally, the root of my hat's brim made of staple fiber ripped. Rain pattered down from time to time. Black clouds thinly covered the sky. The wave undulations increased and sprayed our cheeks as we walked down the narrow path along the coast.

"The roads have gotten much better. They weren't like this six or seven years ago. In a couple of places, you had to wait for a break in the waves and rush through."

"But even now, on a bad night, you can't walk at all."

"Yes, night is bad. It was hard for Yoshitsune and Benkei, too."

We kept our serious looks and kept walking.

"You tired?" N turned and asked, "My legs are surprisingly strong."

"Well, we're not old yet."

After we walked for close to two hours, the scenery became unsettling. It felt dreadful, but that landscape no longer exists. Scenery is seen and described by different people over many years, softens under the gaze of human eyes, and is fed by people. Even at the 318-feet-high Kegon Falls, the scent of people is reminiscent of a caged beast. At famous dangerous places drawn in pictures, recited in songs, chanted in haiku from long ago, without exception, human expression is discovered. But no place along the coast on the northern edge of Honshu becomes scenery. The presence of people in the picture is not allowed.

If people are forced into the scene, an Ainu elder wearing traditional white elm-bark clothing must be borrowed. A dandy man dressed in a purple jacket is pushed away without a second thought and will not be found in pictures or songs. There will be only rocks and water. Perhaps it was Goncharov who once encountered a storm while crossing the ocean, the experienced ship's captain said, "Please come out on deck. How would you describe this huge wave? You're a man of letters and can surely find a remarkable adjective for that wave." Goncharov looked at the wave, sighed, and spoke one word, "Terrifying."

Similar to being unable to imagine any literary adjective for the raging waves of the ocean or the violent winds of the desert, the rocks or water in treacherous places in Honshu are simply terrifying. I looked away from those places and walked only staring at my feet. Around thirty minutes later we arrived in Tappi, I weakly laughed and said, "We're finally here. It would have been nice if we saved some sake. I doubt there's sake at an inn in Tappi. And I'm freezing," I grumbled in spite of myself.

"I had that thought, too. We can go a little further to the home of an old friend who may have sake rations. No one drinks at his house."

"Please try."

"Okay, we cannot be without sake."

His friend's home was in the hamlet right before Tappi. N removed his hat and entered the home. In a short time, he came out with a face trying not to smile.

"Looks like our luck has not run out. He filled one water bottle for me. It's close to a liter."

"The reason is the charcoal remained. Let's go."

We had a little further to go. We bent over against the strong wind and jogged to Tappi. N thrust his head into a chicken coop where the road seemed to be narrowing. I didn't understand why at the time.

"This is Tappi," said N in a changed tone.

"Here?" I said unperturbed and looked around. It felt like a chicken coop, namely, the hamlet of Tappi. The small houses stood in a firm clump against savage winds and rain and protected each other. This place was an extreme end of Honshu. After leaving this hamlet, there are no roads. There's only a drop into the sea. The road vanishes. This is Honshu's dead end. Reader, do not forget this. My friends, when you walk north and take a road somewhere and go uphill. If you keep climbing, you will always reach the Sotogahama Road, and the road finally narrows. If you go further up, you will fall into a mysterious world resembling these tightly packed chicken coops. All roads end there.

"Anyone would be surprised. When I first came here, I even considered entering a stranger's kitchen because I was getting cold," said N.

This is critical land in the nation's defense, so I must avoid saying any more about this hamlet. An old woman came out and led us to a room. The room in this inn was also surprisingly neat and tidy, and the construction was not flimsy. We changed into the quilted nightgowns, sat cross-legged with the hearth between us, and regained tranquility.

"Excuse me, is there any sake?" N asked the old woman in a wise, measured tone. Her response was unexpected.

"Yes, there is," said the woman graced with an oval, elegant face. Relieved by her answer, N smiled and said, "In truth Ma'am, we'd like to drink a bit."

"Go right ahead. Drink as much as you like," she said smiling.

We exchanged glances. I suspected this old woman may not have known how precious alcohol was around that time.

"Today, we have rations. Since most of the homes nearby don't drink, I collect them," she said and moved her hands as in gathering and then spread her arms as if holding many half-gallon bottles, "Before I had this much."

"That much is a lot," I said quite relieved, "I'm sorry to bother you, but could you warm the sake in an iron kettle and pour it into four or five, no, six bottles and bring them as fast as you can."

I thought it'd be better to have her bring many more before she changed her mind.

"We can eat later."

As requested, the old woman brought six bottles of sake and placed them on the tray. Before we finished off two bottles, she came with the meal.

"Here you are. Enjoy."

"Thank you."

The six bottles of sake were gone in no time.

"They're all gone," I said in shock, "Gone in a flash. That was too fast."

"We drank that much," said N looking doubtful and shook an empty bottle, "It's empty. Well, it is cold, and we gulped them down."

"Each bottle nearly overflowed with sake. We drank them so fast, if I ask for six more, she may suspect we're supernatural beings. We can't create unneeded fear by asking for more sake, so let's warm up the sake we brought with us. We'll wait a bit and then ask for only six more. Why shouldn't we drink the night away in this inn at the northern tip of Honshu."

I proposed this queer strategy, which became the foundation of my failure.

We transferred the sake in the water bottles to the sake bottles but drank as slowly as we could. N quickly got drunk.

"I can't do it. Tonight, I may get drunk."

May get drunk? He was already plastered.

"I can't do this. Tonight, I'm getting drunk. Okay? Can I?"

"It won't bother me. I intend to get drunk tonight, too. Let's take our time."

"Why don't I recite a poem? You've probably never heard me recite. I seldom do. But tonight I want to recite one poem. Hey, you can recite one, too."

"I guess I'll have to listen," I said and prepared myself.

N closed his eyes and softly began to recite the usual poem by Bokusui about going to mountains and rivers. It wasn't as bad as I imagined. I listened without a word and was touched.

"Well? Was it weird?"

"No, it was a bit sentimental."

"Well then, another."

Now, this one was awful. His startling, harsh voice shouted, "Did I come to an inn at the tip of Honshu, and my heart swelled?"

He began to recite the poem by Ishikawa Takuboku *On a rocky beach on a small island in the eastern sea*, but his loud, grating voice canceled the sounds of the wind outside.

If I said, "Horrible," he'd say, "That bad? Well, I'll try again," take a deep breath and raise his grating voice again.

"On a small island on a rocky beach in the eastern sea."

This time he jumbled the poem and, for some unknown reason and with no warning, launched into the tale *Masukagami* as if written in the present and the past. He seemed to groan, shriek, and scream. It was awful. I was nervous and thought it'd be better if the old woman inside didn't hear. As I expected, the sliding door opened wide and the old woman came in.

She said, "Oh, you are reciting a poem, but it'll soon be time for bed."

She brought in a tray and deftly spread out the futons. His generous but harsh voice scared the wits out of her. I thought about drinking more, but that turned out to be a stupid idea.

"That was bad. The poem was bad. One or two are enough. More than that would shock anyone," I said displeased but meekly acquiesced.

The next morning, I listened in bed to the enchanting singing voice of a little girl. The winds had quieted down, and the morning sun shined into the room. The girl was on the street in front singing the handball song. I raised my head to listen.

> Se-se-se
> Summer is near
> Eighty-eight nights
> In the fields and in the mountains
> Waves of wisteria blooms in winds
>   of green leaves
> Time for having fun

I found it irresistible. Until now, I never thought I would hear an invigorating song with these beautiful tones in the northern tip of Honshu thought of as the land of the Ezo and held in contempt by people from the center of the country. According to an explanation by Professor Sato:

To speak of the people of current-day Oshu, the pent-up power of emergence seen in Italy before the Renaissance must be recognized in the land of Oshu. In culture and in industry, the generous heart related to the education of the gracious Meiji Emperor permeated all of Oshu in no time. The sounds peculiar to the people of Oshu are unpleasant to hear. Reduction in the nasal sounds and adoption of the standard language are promoted. The light of civilization is given and already seen in the lands that are home to the uncivilized, savage tribes of the Ezo who sunk to their previous primitive state.

I felt light resembling dawn filled with hope in the singing voice of that lovely girl and found it irresistible.

4

THE TSUGARU PLAIN

Tsugaru The former name of the region at the northeastern end of Honshu bordering the Sea of Japan. In the age of Empress Kogyoku (642-645, 655-661), the provincial governor of the Koshi province administered the Ezo lands in the Dewa region, the home of Abe no Hirafu; his reach extended to Akita, Nushiro (today's Noshiro), and Tsugaru, and eventually reached Hokkaido. This was the first appearance of the name Tsugaru, that is, the chief of this land ruled the Tsugaru district. On this occasion, the Japanese envoy to Tang Dynasty China, Sakaibe no Iwashiki, mentioned the Ezo to the Tang emperor.

The accompanying government official, Yuki no Muraji Hakatoko, described the Ezo tribes in response to questions. The closest of the three tribes was called the Nigi Ezo, next the Ara Ezo, and the furthest the Tsugaru. Naturally, the other Ezo were recognized as distinct tribes. The name of the Tsugaru Ezo was seen here and there at the time of the rebellion of the Ebisu of Dewa in the second year of the Gangyo era (878). At that time,

Shogun Fujiwara no Yasunori put down the rebellion, reached Watarijima island from Tsugaru, and previous generations of mixed natives never returned and all came under the jurisdiction of the state. Watarijima is today's Hokkaido. In Mutsu in Tsugaru, Minamoto no Yoritomo controlled Ou and came under the protection of Mutsu.

Origin of Aomori Prefecture The land of this prefecture is a unified province consolidating the lands of the Iwate, Miyagi, and Fukushima Prefectures until the first year of the Meiji era and called Mutsu. In the first year of Meiji, the Mutsu Province had the five domains of Hirosaki, Kuroishi, Hachinohe, Shichinohe, and Tonami. In July of Meiji year 4, many feudal clans were abolished, and all became prefectures. In September of that year, the administration and jurisdiction districts were abolished and reorganized. All five districts were temporarily combined into Hirosaki Prefecture, but Hirosaki Prefecture was abolished in November, Aomori Prefecture was established and given jurisdiction over the domains mentioned above. Later, Ninohe was made a part of Iwate Prefecture and remains so today.

The Tsugaru Clan This clan originated in the Fujiwara clan. The eighth generation Hidei from Shogun in Defense of the North ruled over the land of Mutsu, Tsugaru District during the Kouwa era, and later came to live in the castle in the harbor on Lake Jusan in Tsugaru. Tsugaru became the clan. During the Meiou era, Masanobu, the son of Konoe Hisamichi, became the heir. The clan achieved distinction with Tamenobu, the grandson of Masanobu. The grandson created a branch family and was the origin of various families mainly in the domains of Hirosaki and Kuroishi.

Tsugaru Tamenobu A shogun during the *Sengoku* (warring states) period. His father was Oura Jinzaburo Morinobu. His mother was a daughter of Takeda Shigenobu, the lord of the Horikoshi Castle. He was born in January of Tenmon year 19 (1550). His childhood name was Ougi. In March of year 10 of Eiroku (1567), when he was eighteen years old, he was adopted by his uncle Tsugaru Tamenori and became a nephew of Konoe Sakihisa. His wife was a daughter of Tamenori. In May of year 2 of Genki (1571), he fought and killed Nanbu Takanobu. On July 27 in year 6 of Tensho (1578), he attacked Kitabatake Akiramura, the lord of Namioka Castle, consolidated the domain, plundered nearby villages, and unified Tsugaru in year 13. Two years later, he sought an audience with Toyotomi Hideyoshi and left for Edo. Abe Sunesue, the mediator at Akita Castle, blocked the road and turned him back.

In year 17, he gifted a hawk and a horse to Hideyoshi in goodwill. And during the Siege of Odawara in year 18, he supported Hideyoshi's army and provided relief to Tsugaru, Ainoura, and Sotogahama. During the Kunohe Rebellion in year 19, he dispatched soldiers. In April of Bunroku year 2 (1593), he had an audience with Hideyoshi and an audience with the Konoe clan, and in January of year 3 given the lower rank of *Jushii Ugyou no Daifu*. In the fifth year of Keicho (1600) in Sekigahara, he dispatched soldiers and accompanied the army of Tokugawa Ieyasu and went west to fight in Ogaki, and was given a stipend increase of 2,000 koku and Odate in the Kozuke Province. On December 5 of year 12, Tsugaru Tamenobu died in Kyoto at the age of fifty-eight.

Tsugaru Plain This plain is located in the Mutsu Province extending over the southern, central, and northern Tsugaru districts and forms the river valley of the Iwaki River. The east is fenced in by the mountains forming the backbone of the Tsugaru Peninsula running north and west of Lake Towada. The south demarcates the watershed from Yatatetoge and Tateishigoe in Ugosakai. The west is protected by the mountain cluster of Mount Iwaki and a belt of sand dunes (called Mount Byobusan) on the coastline. Iwaki River flowing from its foundation in the west, Hira River flowing from the south, and Asaseishi River flowing from the east meet north of Hirosaki City and flow due north and into the sea after pouring into Lake Jusan. The expanse of the plain runs thirty-six miles north to south and twelve miles east to west and narrows in the northward direction. The seven miles along the line from Kizukuri to Goshogawara and just two miles when the shore of Jusan is reached. The low-lying land in this plain threaded by a network of tributary canals produce most of the rice in Aomori Prefecture.

(from *The Great Encyclopedia of Japan*)

Few people know the history of Tsugaru. Some believe Mutsu and Aomori Prefecture are the same as Tsugaru. Understandably, we glimpse the noun *Tsugaru* in only one place, in the textbooks on the history of Japan we learned from in school. A description of the conquest of Ezo by Abe no Hirafu reads, "Upon the death of Emperor Kotoku, Empress Kogyoku ascended the throne. The Imperial Prince Nakano no Oe succeeded her. As crown prince, he assisted in governing and appointed Abe no Hirafu to subjugate the lands of what is now Akita and Tsugaru."

The name Tsugaru appears no more. In grammar

Home to Tsugaru

school textbooks, middle school textbooks, and high school textbooks, the name Tsugaru never appeared other than with references to Hirafu. The dispatch of governor-generals in the 573 years of the imperial era reached north to the area of today's Fukushima Prefecture. For the next two hundred years, the pacification of the Ezo by Yamato-takeru of Japan reached north to the Hitakami Province, which is now the northern region of Miyagi Prefecture. After five hundred fifty years passed, the Taiki Reform came. Through the subjugation of Ezo by Abe no Hirafu, the name Tsugaru began to float up but then sank. The name Tsugaru does not promptly emerge except in discussions of the construction of Taga Castle (now near Sendai City) and Akita Castle (now Akita City), and the subjugation of Ezo during the Nara period.

When the Heian period (794-1185) was entered, Sakanoue no Tamuramaro advanced far north and destroyed the Ezo base and built Isawa Castle (now the neighborhood of Mizusawa-cho in Iwate Prefecture) as the garrison but did not go as far as Tsugaru. Later, the expedition of Funya no Watamaro took place during the Konin years (810-824). And in year 2 of Gangyo, Dewa and Ezo revolted, and Fujiwara Gensoku went to pacify them. The Tsugaru Ezo were said to have aided in the revolts. We may not be experts, but in the subjugation of the Ezo, Tamuramaro is mentioned. The next two hundred fifty years flew by. Its roles are taught about only the Former Nine Years War and the Later Three Years War at the beginning of the Gempei period.

These wars took place in Iwate Prefecture and Akita Prefecture. Only the Abe clan and the Kiyohara clan, the so-called Nigi Ezo, were active. Little is written in our textbooks about the actions of trueborn Ezo in the backcountry called Tsugaru. Then for three generations of the

Fujiwara clan, over one hundred years, was the golden age of Hiraizumi. In the year 5 of Bunji (1189), Oshu was pacified by Minamoto no Yoritomo. From that era on, our textbooks finally reach beyond the Tohoku region. During the Meiji Restoration, various clans of Oshu stood up, straightened the hems of their kimonos, and sat back down. The gumption found in clans of the provinces of Satsuma and Choshu was not seen in them.

Although it is written they took advantage of the spirit of the age with no major blunders, they had no choice. As a result, there is nothing. Our textbooks tell of ancient times from Emperor Jimmu until modern times, sadly, the name *Tsugaru* can only be found once, Abe no Hirafu. What happened in Tsugaru during that time? Only the straightening of kimonos and sitting down again and again. For two thousand, six hundred years, did they never take one step outside and only blinked their eyes? No, that's not so. If the parties involved were asked, they would say something like "It may look that way, but we're terribly busy."

> Ou is the combination of Oshu and Dewa. Oshu is an abbreviation of Mutsu. Mutsu was the general term for Shirakawa and Nakoso north of Niseki. The name *Michi no oku* is abbreviated to *Michinoku*. The pronunciation of *Michi*, the name of the country, was *Mutsu* in the ancient regional sounds. This region received the ends of the Tokai and Toyama Roads and was the innermost country of a different race and called nothing other than the vague Michi-no-oku (end of the road). The kanji for *Michi* means road.
>
> Next, Dewa is *Idewa* and is interpreted to mean *Idewashi* (go outside). Long ago, the land on the Sea of Japan side of Honshu from the central region to

Tohoku was vaguely called the province of Koshi. This was also in the interior and, similar to Michinoku, was the benighted land of another race beyond imperial rule and called Idewashi. In other words, the name shows that Mutsu bordering the Pacific Ocean was remote land forever outside the emperor's rule.

That was Professor Kita Sadakichi's concise explanation. An explanation is best when concise and clear. Because the Dewa and Oshu provinces were regarded as remote lands, they may have been considered the habitats of bears and monkeys reaching to the northern tip of the Tsugaru Peninsula. Professor Kita further explains the history of Dewa and Oshu. The article is as follows.

Although after the subjugation of Ou by Yoritomo, they were unable to naturally unify under his rule. Based on the reason of "from the land of Ebisu in Dewa and Mutsu," the reforms of the field system recently implemented had to be canceled, and all the old regulations of Hidehira and of Yasuhira had to be followed.

Accordingly, similar to the northernmost Tsugaru region, the predicament appeared to be most of the residents lived in the old way of the Ezo but were directly ruled by Kamakura samurai. A wealthy, local Ando clan was appointed the magistrate and suppressed the people as the administrator of Ezo.

From the time of the Ando clan, little was known of the situation in Tsugaru. Before then, the Ainu may have been loafing around. However, these Ainu cannot be mocked and are a type of the so-called indigenous people of Japan. However, the Ainu remaining in Hokkaido now seem to fundamentally have a different nature.

Looking at their relics and ruins, they were said to be far superior to all the unglazed earthenware of the Stone Age. The ancestors of the Ainu in Hokkaido today have lived there since ancient times. With little contact with the culture of Honshu, the land was isolated and had few natural resources. Thus, in the Stone Age, the same tribe of the Ou region showed no development. Especially in the modern era, since the Matsumae clan, they often suffered oppression by the Japanese people from the interior and were broken. In contrast to reaching the apex of depravity, the Ainu of Ou were actively proud of their independent culture and migrated to provinces in the interior but gradually became Yamato people indistinguishable from the other regions as more Japanese people poured into Ou.

Professor Ogawa Takuji came to the following conclusions.

> The classical text *Shoku Nihongi* states around the beginning of the Nara era, the Sushen people and the Bokkai people crossed the Sea of Japan. The most remarkable migration was more than one thousand Bokkai people migrated in Tenpyo year 18 (1406) of Emperor Shomu and Houki year 2 (1431) of Emperor Konin. Next, a large number of people exceeding three hundred arrived in what is now the Akita region. It is not difficult to imagine they freely crossed into the Oshu region. *Goshusen* coins have been excavated in the Akita area. There seem to be shrines enshrining Emperor Wen and Emperor Wu of China in Tohoku. This suggests direct traffic between the continent and this region.
>
> Present-day and old stories tell of the crossing of the Emishi ruler Abe no Yoritoki to Manchuria. By also considering archeological and ethnographic data, these

stories should not be discarded as scenes from folk tales. We move one step forward. Since coming under imperial rule and the eastern advance, we are convinced based on conclusions drawn from the sparse historical data remaining in central Japan that the extent of civilization acquired by the tribes at that time through direct contact with the continent was not insignificant. Shoguns like Tamuramaro, Yoriyoshi, and Yoshiie had great difficulty quashing these tribes. They were first dispelled of the idea that their rivals were simply ignorant and not like the fearless, savage tribes of Taiwan.

Professor Ogawa found it interesting to think the names often given to these people by the officials of the Yamato court such as Emishi, Azumabito (people of the east), and Kebito (hairy people) have meanings favoring the courage or the chic, exotic emotions of the people of Ou. From that perspective, the ancestors of the people of Tsugaru were certainly not loafing around at the tip of Honshu but are not depicted in the history of central Japan.

From the Ando clan described above, the situation in Tsugaru is well understood. Professor Kita reasons:

The Ando clan is called the descendants of the son Takaboshi of Abe no Sadato. A distant ancestor is said to be Abi, the older brother of Negasunehiko, the chieftain who battled Emperor Jimmu, the first emperor of Japan, and given the death penalty. Abi went to Sotogahama in Oshu; his descendants are said to be the Abe clan. In any case, before the Kamakura era, this clan was powerful in northern Ou. In Tsugaru, the three districts at the entry were in service to Kamakura. The inner three districts were lands controlled by the imperial household and lands with no role and not registered in the *Registry of the Nation*. The influence of the Kamakura shogunate did not reach these remote interior lands, but by relying on the freedom of the Ando clan, these lands became the so-called protected and untraveled lands.

At the end of the Kamakura era, internal discord erupted among the families of the Ando clan in Tsugaru and led to riots by the Ezo. Houjou Takatori, a regent of the shogunate, sent a shogun to suppress the riots. The power of the Kamakura samurai did not lead to victory, but in the end, was saved through compromise.

As expected, Professor Kita explained Tsugaru's history with an air of scant confidence. The history of Tsugaru may not be fully known. This province at the northern tip fought other provinces and appears to have never been defeated. They appeared to have no conception of submission. The shoguns of the other provinces were astounded and pretended not to see this and acted as they pleased. They resemble literary circles in the Showa era. Aside from that, they did not make alliances with other provinces, quarreled internally with their comrades, and started fighting.

One example is a riot of the Tsugaru Ezo triggered by internal strife in one family of the Ando clan. Among the Tsugaru people, according to *A Brief History of Aomori Prefecture* by Takeuchi Umpei:

> ... strife in the Ando clan led to riots in the eight provinces of Kanto and became 'the beginning of the crisis that would alter life in heaven and on earth' noted in the historical record *Houjou Kudai-ki* (A Record of the Nine Generations of the Houjou) and led to the Genko Inci-

dent and the restoration during the Kenmu era (1333-1336).

Perhaps, it should be counted as one of the remote causes of that major undertaking. In truth, Tsugaru affected, although slight, the politics of central Japan. The discord in the Ando clan must be a glorious record deserving special mention in the history of Tsugaru.

The area near the Pacific Ocean in today's Aomori Prefecture was Ezo land long known as Nukanobu. After the Kamakura period, the Nanbu clan, a branch of the Takeda clan in Koshu, migrated here and became powerful, and after the Yoshino and Muromachi eras passed, achieved unification of the entire country under Hideyoshi. Tsugaru fought Nanbu. In place of the Ando clan, the Tsugaru clan was established in Tsugaru and somehow calmed the entire province of Tsugaru. In the twelfth generation of the Tsugaru clan during the Meiji Restoration, the feudal lord Tsuguakira respectfully ceded the domain to the emperor. That's an outline of the history of Tsugaru. There are various theories about remote ancestors of this Tsugaru clan.

Professor Kita also touched on this.

> In Tsugaru, the Ando clan fell. The Tsugaru clan gained independence and was long viewed as the enemy by the Nanbu clan. Their domain abutted the boundary with the Nanbu clan. The Tsugaru clan was said to descend from Konoe Hisamichi, a chief adviser to the emperor, or may be a branch of the Nanbu clan or descendants of the second son Hideshige of Fujiwara Motohira or a branch family in the Ando clan.

Also, Takeuchi Umpei explained the following about this issue.

The Nanbu family and the Tsugaru family passed through and felt great alienation the entire time. The origin of the above was the Nanbu clan considered the Tsugaru clan to be enemies of their ancestors for appropriating their former fief. The Tsugaru clan was originally a branch of the Nanbu and resisted the lord from the ranks of low-level government officials. On the other hand, the Tsugaru clan claimed the Fujiwara clan as their ancestors and emphasized the addition of the bloodlines of the Konoe clan even in medieval times.

In fact, Nanbu Takanobu was overthrown to benefit Tsugaru Tamenobu and had various castles seized in the southern part of Tsugaru. The mothers of the ancestors of Oura Mitsunobu for several generations of Tamenobu were women with the pedigree of Nanbu Kuji Bizen-no-kami and the next few generations had the courtesy title of *Nanbu Shinano-no-kami*. It's reasonable to believe these women harbored hatred toward the Tsugaru family of the Nanbu clan as traitors. The Tsugaru family searched for distant ancestors among the Fujiwara and Konoe clans. In the present day, convincing foundational proof does not necessarily exist.

Feeble arguments are presented as in the *Record of Kasoku* that does not defend the Nanbu clan. As the *Record of the Takaya Clan* long ago states about Tsugaru, the Oura clan is a branch family of the Nanbu clan. *Kidate's Diary* also states "The families of Nanbu and Tsugaru become one body." In contrast to recently-published books like *Tokushi Biyou* (A History Reader) that state Tamenobu lived as part of the Kuji clan (family in the Nanbu clan), data does not exist today to verify the correctness of this assertion. However, the Nanbu have lineage in Tsugaru in the past. Even as low-ranking government officials, it cannot be said there is no history from any perspective other than the family line.

Similar to this statement from Professor Kita, a firm conclusion is avoided. I mentioned at the beginning of this chapter for reference what is stipulated directly and unequivocally by the *Nihon Daihyakka Daijiten* (The Great Encyclopedia of Japan).

The above description flowed, but on a closer look, Tsugaru has an insignificant existence from the perspective of Japan as a whole. In *Oku no Hosomichi* (Narrow Road to the Deep North) by Basho, he writes of his departure, "Thoughts of traveling three thousand *ri* before me fills my heart." North was Hiraizumi at that time and is no further than the southern edge of Iwate Prefecture today. It would take twice as much walking to reach Aomori Prefecture. Tsugaru is one peninsula on the Sea of Japan side of Aomori Prefecture. The Tsugaru of old was centered on the Tsugaru Plain that extended along the Iwaki River flowing over sixty miles; to the east were Aomori and the Asamushi area; to the west were the shores on the Sea of Japan; the north went down along the shore to the Fukaura area; and the south probably reached Hirosaki.

The Kuroishi clan, a branch family, lived in the south and had a tradition of independence as the Kuroishi clan in this area and encouraged what could be called a cultural temperament different from that of the Tsugaru clan. Now, in the north is Tappi and its narrowness is disheartening. It's reasonable for Tappi to go unmentioned in the history of central Japan. I spent the night in an inn deep in the north in *Narrow Road to the Deep North*. The next day, the boat didn't leave port. The road I walked the previous day took me to Minmaya. I ate lunch there then returned by bus to N's home in Kanita. On foot, Tsugaru isn't so small.

About noon two days later, I left Kanita alone by ferry and arrived at Aomori Port at three in the afternoon. I traveled by the Ou line to Kawabe, changed to the Gono Line, arrived in Goshogawara around five, and immediately took the Tsugaru Railway north over the Tsugaru Plain. The light was already dim when I arrived in Kanagi, the place of my birth. Kanita and Kanagi are a distance from each other and follow one side of a rectangle. Lying between them is the Bonjusan mountain range where nothing resembled a path. There's no choice but to take a huge detour along the other three sides of the rectangle. I arrived at my birth home and first went to the Buddhist altar room. My older brother's wife came with me and opened wide the door to the altar room. For a time, I gazed at the photographs of my parents on the altar and respectfully bowed. Then I went to the family sitting room to greet my sister-in-law again.

"When did you leave Tokyo?" she asked.

A few days before leaving Tokyo, I sent a postcard to my sister-in-law stating that I was thinking about touring Tsugaru and planning to stop by Kanagi to visit my parents' graves and hoped that wouldn't be an imposition.

"About a week ago. I was delayed on the eastern shore. N from Kanita was a great help."

She must know about N and said, "Oh, I see. I received your postcard and wondered if something had happened and worried when you didn't appear. Yoko and Mitsu have been waiting for you and went to the railway station every day. In the end, someone became cross and said she wouldn't notice even if you came."

Yoko is the oldest daughter of my oldest brother. About

six months earlier she married into the family of a landowner near Hirosaki but visited Kanagi from time to time with her groom. The couple was visiting at that time. Mitsu is the youngest daughter of my oldest sister. Still unmarried, she always comes to help at the house in Kanagi and is an obedient child. These two nieces clinging to each other came laughing cheerfully to greet their uncle, the undisciplined drinker. Yoko looked like a student and not in the least like someone's wife.

"You look ridiculous," they immediately said and laughed at my clothes.

"You dopes. This is popular in Tokyo."

Assisted by my sister-in-law, my grandmother appeared. She was eighty-eight.

"Oh wonderful, you came. You came," she shouted. She was energetic although she looked weak shuffling in.

"What shall we do?" asked my sister-in-law looking at me, "Shall we eat here? The others are on the second floor."

Yoko's groom was seated between my two oldest brothers. They were just starting to drink on the second floor.

How much etiquette is maintained among brothers? And what degree of candidness and rudeness is acceptable? I still have no idea.

"Would it be a problem if I went upstairs?"

I thought it'd be unpleasant if I drank beer here alone and would look meek.

"Either is fine," she said smiling then gave an order to the young women, "Well, take the cups upstairs."

Wearing my jacket, I went upstairs to the nicest room with golden papered sliding doors. My brothers were quietly drinking when I made my noisy entrance.

"Hello, I'm Shuji. Pleased to meet you."

First, I greeted the groom then apologized to my

brothers for being away for so long. Both brothers gave a short grunt and nodded in consent. That is the way in our family. No, you could say it's the way in Tsugaru. I'm used to it. Mitsu and my sister-in-law calmly poured sake into the cups, and I drank the sake in silence. The son-in-law was sitting behind the alcove post, and his face was flushed bright red. My brothers had always been strong drinkers but seemed much weaker.

"Here, would you like more?"

"No, I'm fine, thank you."

"And you?"

In this way, we politely went back and forth. After my wild drinking in Sotogahama, coming here was like entering the Palace of the Sea God or a different world. I was shocked and nervous about the gulf between the lives of my brothers and mine.

"Shall we have the crabs later?" whispered my sister-in-law. I brought crabs as a gift from Kanita.

"Uh."

I hesitated because crabs are a little too rustic for the elegant bowls. My sister-in-law may have felt the same.

"Crabs?" asked my oldest brother, "Don't worry. Bring them. And bring napkins."

The mood that night might have been pleasant in the absence of my brothers and the son-in-law.

The crabs arrived.

"Please, help yourself," my oldest brother offered them first to the son-in-law and shelled the crabs.

I sighed with relief.

"Excuse me, but who are you?" the son-in-law asked me with an innocent, smiling look on his face. I was startled but immediately reconsidered and found the question understandable.

"Oh, you see, I am the brother after Eiji (the name of

my second oldest brother)," I said smiling but was disheartened. I felt craven by having to use Eiji's name. I gauged Eiji's reaction, but he looked indifferent and I felt cut adrift. No, that's not true, I sat relaxed and had Mitsu pour more beer for me.

The mood in my home in Kanagi is mental fatigue. I will be unable to write about this later. A man burdened by the bad karma of writing about his relatives and then not being able to sell the manuscript is gifted by the gods with this birthplace. In the end, I nap in a hovel in Tokyo and longed to see the dreams of home. I'll probably linger here and there and then die.

The next day, it rained. I got up and went to my oldest brother's drawing room. He was showing the son-in-law a picture. The golden folding screen had two parts decorated with elegant scenes. On one was drawn a wild cherry blossom tree. On the other was the landscape of the countryside. I saw the artist's seal and signature but couldn't read them.

"Who's this by?" I timidly asked while blushing.

"Suian," said my brother.

"Suian," I said still clueless.

"You don't know him?" said my brother, calmly without scolding, "He is the father of Hyakusui."

"Really?"

Of course, I heard that the father of Hirafuku Hyakusui was an artist but did not know the father Suisan drew such fine pictures. It's not that I don't like paintings. I'm not knowledgeable about paintings. I don't hate them. No, if I hate anything, it is my intention to become an authority. My great blunder was I never heard of Suian. My eyes saw the folding screen and I was in awe. If I whispered Suian, my brother may have viewed me differently. I regret asking, "Who's this by?" in a dopey voice. I agonized over the fact that could not be undone. Taking no notice of me, my brother said quietly to the son-in-law, "He's a celebrated artist in Akita."

"You could say he is like Ayatari of Tsugaru," I said timidly to redeem my honor and to flatter. The painters of Tsugaru are in the same class as Ayatari. In fact, on an earlier visit to Kanagi, my brother showed me a painting by Ayatari he owned. That was the first time I knew Tsugaru had an artist this great.

"Well, he's different," said my brother sounding completely uninterested and sat on a chair. The son-in-law and I stood gazing at the paintings on the folding screen, but my brother took a seat. The son-in-law sat in the opposite chair. I sat on the sofa beside the door a slight distance away.

"This man, it seems, has this as his main theme," said my brother to the son-in-law of course. My brother rarely spoke directly to me.

With him saying this, given his feelings on the significance of Ayatari, he seemed a little troubled by Ayatari's work falling into simple folk art.

"What is cultural tradition?" asked my brother as he rounded his back and stared at the son-in-law, "Naturally, the roots are deep in Akita."

"Is Tsugaru bad?"

No matter what I said, the result was awkward, and I gave up and talked to myself.

My brother surprised me with a question, "What will you write about Tsugaru this time?"

"Oh, well, I don't know much about Tsugaru," I said stumbling, "Are there any good reference books?"

"Let's see," said my brother smiling, "I have little interest in local history."

"There are probably popular guidebooks about famous sites in Tsugaru. I know absolutely nothing."

"No. None," said my brother shaking his head and smiling as though appalled by my carelessness.

He stood and said to the son-in-law, "I'll be going to the agricultural association for a while to consult some books. The weather will get worse today," then he left.

"Is it busy at the agricultural association around this time of year?" I asked the son-in-law.

"Yes, quite busy. Right now, they're determining the delivery quota for rice," said the son-in-law.

Although young, he was a landowner and well versed in this field. He explained various detailed numbers to me, but I couldn't grasp half of it.

"These days, I don't think seriously about rice. In this age, I gaze alternating between joy and sorrow at the rice fields from the train window as if they were mine. It's been a bit chilly until now this year, so has the rice been planted?"

My habit is to brandish my superficial knowledge at experts.

"It will be all right. If it gets cold around now, it will be cold, and the measures to take will be considered. The seedlings are sprouting normally."

"Is that so?" I said nodding and trying to look like I understood, "My knowledge was gained only from staring at the Tsugaru Plain yesterday from the train window. Now does tilling with horses leave plowing the field to the horse? It often appears to be left to oxen. When I was young, not only horses tilled, but handcarts were used. Everything was done by horses; the oxen helped but almost never plowed. When I first went to Tokyo, I saw oxen pulling carts. It was a strange sight."

"That's true. Horses have become scarce. Most were

sent to war. This may be related to the ease of raising cattle. But from the perspective of work efficiency, oxen have half the efficiency of horses, no, it's probably much, much worse."

"Going off to war, have you…"

"Me? I've already received two warrants, but I was discharged and sent home both times. It's shameful."

The healthy young man had an untroubled, smiling look on his face. He said in a breezy, natural tone, "I don't want to be discharged the next time."

"Are there great men worthy of heartfelt praise hidden in this land?"

"I'm not sure, but they may be found among the hard-working farmers?"

"Yes, that's true."

I wholeheartedly agreed.

"My reasoning is sloppy, but we'd like to live with the single-minded determination of industrious farmers. However, we have petty vanity and, in practice, end up smug. But isn't it harmful to stamp farmers with a cumbersome label like industrious farmers?"

"That's true. The newspaper companies irresponsibly raised a clamor and dragged them out to be lectured and ended up turning the valuable, hard-working farmers into strange men. Nothing good happens when they become famous."

"That's right," I said in sympathy, "Man is a sorrowful creature and has a weakness for fame. Originally, journalism was the invention of capitalists in America and is irresponsible. The moment they become famous, they mostly become simpletons."

I swept away the resentment about my personal matters at a strange place. Although this complainer speaks this way, caution is required because I tend to have the desire in my heart to become famous.

A little past noon, I opened an umbrella and walked alone around the garden in the rain. The plants looked the same. That was unusual, and I guessed it was through the efforts of my brother who maintains the old house. I stood at the edge of the lake and heard a faint sound. I looked and saw a frog jump into the lake. The sound was small and thin. At that moment, I understood Basho's poem about the ancient pond. I never understood that poem before. I could not imagine which part was good. I concluded reality always fell short of the promise because I received a poor education.

What kind of explanation did we receive in school about this poem about the ancient pond? A hushed noon darkness covered the dark blue ancient pond. A frog plopped in there (and did not throw itself into a big river). Ah, we were taught sounds linger, and the bird sings and the mountain becomes quieter. It's probably a lousy poem that is tantalizing but trite. The sarcasm is chilling. For a long time, this poem disgusted me and I kept my distance. Now, I've reconsidered and it's not that bad.

I don't understand the explanation for the plop. There's no reverberation, nothing. Only a simple plop. In other words, it is actually a sparse sound in an obscure corner of the world. A humble sound. Basho heard it and was deeply touched.

> An ancient pond
> A frog jumps in
> The sound of water

When I reconsider this poem, it's not bad. It's a good poem. I capably reject the affected mannerisms of the temple grammar school in those days. That is, it is an exceptional idea. There is no moon, no snow, and no flowers. There is also no elegance.

There is simply the poor life of a poor man. The refined teachers in those days were amazed by this poem and understood it well. The ordinary elegant idea is destroyed. It is a revolution. I got excited and thought it a lie to say good artists like this do not appear. This is what I wrote that night in my travel diary.

> A rose
> A frog jumps in
> The sound of water

Was that a poem by Kikaku? I don't know.

> Come with me
> An orphan sparrow
> Come closer

Frankly, the meaning is awful. The ancient pond has no rival.

The next day, the weather was excellent. My niece Yoko, her husband, Aya, and I set off carrying bento lunches to a small, gently sloping mountain no taller than two hundred meters called Takanagare located about two and a half miles east of Kanagi. Although named Aya, it is not the name of a woman. It meant an old handyman and is also a substitute for Father. The feminine version of *Aya* is *Apa*. She's also called *Aba*. I have no idea where these words came from. My guess is they came from the dialect words of *Oya* and *Oba*. Various *experts* probably offer a myriad of explanations. According to my niece, the correct pronunciation of the mountain's name of Takanagare is

Takanagane. The name comes from the expansive, gently sloping skirt of the mountain and is said to have the feeling of a long root, *nagane*. But this too may produce various explanations from various experts. The tendency for the assorted explanations from experts to be scattered and fickle is the charm of local history.

My niece and Aya were delayed in preparing the bento, so the son-in-law and I left the house a little before them. The weather was nice. Excursions in Tsugaru are limited to May and June. *Toyuki* comments about travelers:

> From long ago, everyone goes north for pleasure in the summer. When the plants are colored green, the winds change to southerly winds, and the surface of the sea is calm. It does not live up to its terrible reputation. If I reach the northern region sometime between September and March, I will meet absolutely no travelers. The sole exception is traveling for the practice of medicine. In this country, people who come in the spirit of searching out only famous sites should always arrive after April.

The reader should take this to heart.

Around this time, the flowers on plum, peach, cherry blossom, apple, pear, and Chinese plum trees bloom once a year in Tsugaru. With confidence, I led the way to the outskirts of town but did not know the way to Takanagare. I went two or three times during my grammar school days and thought forgetting the way was reasonable. However, the area was completely different from what I remember. I was embarrassed.

"Where's the station? This area looks totally different. I have no clue about the best way to Takanagare. Which one is the mountain?" I asked as I looked straight ahead and pointed at a pale green hill rising in the shape of an upside-down V. I smiled and made a suggestion to the son-in-law.

"We'll wait here a while for Aya and your wife."

"Yes, let's do that," said the son-in-law, also smiling, "I heard the Aomori Prefecture Experimental Farm is in this area."

He knew more than I.

"Really? Let's look for it," I said.

The experimental farm was at the top of a small hill about a mile off the road on the right. It was established to train the rural workers and pioneers forming the backbone of agriculture. However, facilities that are almost too good were set up in the wilderness in the northern tip of Honshu. Chichibu-no-miya, the younger brother of the emperor, served in the Eighth Division in Hirosaki and graciously gave substantial assistance to this experimental farm. They are also indebted to him for the auditorium, a solemn building rarely seen in the area, as well as workshops, livestock sheds, fertilizer depots, and boarding houses. My eyes opened wide in amazement.

"What? I had no idea. Isn't this a bit much for Kanagi?" I said and was oddly overjoyed. I was secretly zealous about the land of my birth.

A large stone monument stood at the entrance to the farm respectfully inscribed with its repeated honors.

Visited by Asaka-no-miya-sama, August of Showa year 10 (1935)

Visited by Takamatsu-no-miya-sama, September of Showa year 10

Visited by Chichibu-no-miya and Doko-no-miya-sama, October of Showa year 10

Visited again by Chichibu-no-miya, August of Showa year 13

The people of Kanagi are right to be proud of the experimental farm. Not only Kanagi, this should be the eternal pride of the Tsugaru Plain. The training lands of crop fields, orchards, and rice paddies behind the buildings were created by model rural youth selected from each hamlet in Tsugaru and were developed to be truly beautiful. The son-in-law walked around and inspected the cultivated fields.

"This is very important," he said and sighed. As a landowner, he understood much more than I.

"Ah! Fuji is great!" I shouted. It was not the Mount Fuji, but the 1,625-meter-high Mount Iwaki, also called Tsugaru Fuji, rising gently where the paddy fields stretching as far as the eye can see came to an end. It actually seemed to be rising. The skirt of the ceremonial dress of a lady of the court, more feminine than Mount Fuji, appeared to drip a pale white. Scattered gingko leaves were opened as if standing upside-down. The mountain had perfect left-right symmetry and floated in the quiet blue skies. The mountain is not tall but is an attractive woman of nearly translucent beauty.

"Kanagi isn't so bad," I said in a hurried tone and then pouting said, "Not bad at all."

"It is nice," calmly said the son-in-law.

I saw Tsugaru Fuji from various sides on this trip. From Hirosaki, it is massive and ponderous. On the one hand, I thought Mount Iwaki may be a part of Hirosaki but was unable to forget the fragile form on the side of Mount Iwaki seen from Kanagi, Goshogawara, and Kizukuri on the Tsugaru Plain. The profile of the mountain viewed from the western sea coast is awful. It has collapsed and looks nothing like a beautiful woman. In lands where Mount Iwaki looks stunning, the legend is rice ripens well and beautiful women abound. Rice aside, this mountain looks beautiful in northern Tsugaru, but I was dissatisfied by the beautiful women I saw, which may reflect the shallowness of my observations.

"I wonder what happened to Aya and Yoko," I said worried and in a huff, "Maybe they didn't follow right after us."

As worried as I was about them, we admired the facilities and landscape of the experimental farm. We returned to the road and looked all around. Aya unexpectedly popped out of a path in a side field and smiled as he told us they had split up to search for us. Aya searched a nearby field, and Yoko followed behind on a path leading to Takanagare.

"That's awful. Yoko has probably gone quite far. Hey Yoko!" I yelled, but there was no response.

"Let's go," said Aya while hiking up the load on his back, "Well, there's only one road."

Skylarks chirped in the sky. It has probably been twenty years since I walked in the fields of my home in the springtime. Thick growths of low shrubs and bushes were scattered on the grass. There was a small marsh. The ground gently undulated. Long ago, people from the city might have praised it as a splendid golf course.

"Look there, hoes dig in to steadily reclaim this uncultivated field. The roofs of people's homes were dazzling. Those hamlets have been restored and separated from neighboring villages," Aya explained.

While listening, I keenly felt Kanagi has also progressed and livened up. We would soon be approaching the slope but had still not seen Yoko.

"What could have happened to her?" I asked, having inherited the habit of worrying too much from my mother.

"Where could she be?" asked her new husband looking embarrassed.

"Well, let's ask," I said and approached a farmer working in the field beside the road. I removed my cloth hat, bowed, and asked, "Has a young lady dressed in Western clothes passed by on the road?"

He answered yes and said she seemed to be in a hurry. I imagined my niece running down the country road in the spring after her new husband and didn't think that was bad. We were soon climbing the mountain. In the shadow of a line of large trees, my smiling niece stood. She concluded we were behind her because she chased after us this far. While waiting she had gathered bracken fern fronds from the area. She didn't look tired. The area resembled a treasure house of bracken, ginseng, thistle, and bamboo shoots. In the fall, mushrooms like *hatsudake*, earth covering, and *nameko* grow in abundance, "like a blanket" in Aya's description. He said people come to gather them from as far away as Goshogawara and Kizukuri.

"Yoko is famous for collecting mushrooms," he added. While climbing the mountain, I said, "The imperial prince has been to Kanagi."

Aya replied yes in a changed tone.

"That's wonderful."

"Yes," he said nervously.

"He came to a place like Kanagi."

"Yes."

"Did he come by car?"

"Yes, he did."

"You bowed to him, too, Aya."

"Yes, I did."

"That made you happy, Aya."

"Yes," he answered and used the towel wrapped around his neck to wipe the sweat off his face.

Bush warblers were singing. Violets, dandelions, wild

chrysanthemums, azaleas, snow flowers, *akebi*, and other flowers unfamiliar to me bloomed brightly on the grass on both sides of the mountain road. Short willow and oak trees were sprouting. As we climbed the mountain, the bamboo grass thickened. Despite this small mountain being less than two hundred meters high, the view was spectacular. I wanted to say the entire Tsugaru Plain could be seen from corner to corner. We stopped and looked down at the plain. I listened to Aya's description and walked a little then stopped to look with pride at Tsugaru Fuji. We soon reached the peak of this small mountain.

"Is this the peak?" I asked Aya a little blankly.

"Yes, it is."

Although I said, "What is this?" I was fascinated by the scenery of the Tsugaru Plain in the spring unfolding before my eyes. The Iwaki River seemed to glimmer and resembled a fine silver streak. In the area where the silver streak ran out, the dull brightness like an ancient mirror was probably Lake Tappi. The whiteness spreading out like dim smoke in the distance was probably Lake Jusan, which is also called Jusan Lagoon. The record states that

> The nearly thirteen tributaries of big and small rivers in Tsugaru meet in this area to form a huge lake. And here, each river loses its distinct color.

It is also referred to as *Jusan Ourai* (thirteen roads).

In the lake at the northern end of the Tsugaru Plain, beginning with the Iwaki River, thirteen big and small rivers flow through the Tsugaru Plain. The lake's circumference is around twenty miles. However, the lake is shallow because sediment is carried by the river water. Even the deepest part is said to be about three meters. The water is salty due to the inflow of seawater, but the river water flowing in from the Iwaki River is not insignificant. Near the mouth of the river is fresh water and is home to both freshwater and saltwater fish. At the southern mouth where the lake opens to the Sea of Japan is the small hamlet of Jusan.

The area opened up seven to eight hundred years ago and was the base of the powerful Tsugaru and Ando clans. In the Edo period (1603-1868), the wood resources and rice of Tsugaru were shipped from Port Kodomari in the north and made this region prosperous. But today, there is no trace of this. Gongen-zaki is north of Lake Jusan. However, this area is part of a region important to national defense. Our eyes moved further past the Iwaki River in front of us to a vivid line drawn in blue. It was the Sea of Japan. We saw an unbroken view of the coastline of Shichirinagahama. From Gongen-zaki in the north to Odose-zaki in the south, nothing blocked our view.

"This is nice. I would build a castle right here," I started to say.

"What would you do in the winter?" interrupted Yoko then said nothing.

"Well, it must snow," I said a bit downcast and sighed.

We went down to the mountain stream in the shadow of the mountain and opened the bento lunch in the dry riverbed. The beer we cooled in the stream wasn't bad. My niece and Aya drank apple juice. Then out of the blue, I screamed, "Snake! Snake!"

The son-in-law put the jacket he took off under his arm and stood up halfway.

"It's all right. It's safe," I said and pointed to the cliff face on the other side of the mountain stream, "He's crawling up the cliff over there."

I saw his head pop out of the rapids and watched him clamber up the rock face for just one foot and then fall back down. He quickly started to climb up again and fell back again. The tenacious snake tried twenty times and, predictably, tired and quit. His extended body floated on the surface of the water as it was swept away by the current and close to this side of the shore. This time, Aya stood up. He ran over carrying a branch about six feet long and plunged the branch into the stream to stab the snake. We looked away.

"Is it dead? Is it dead?" I asked in a grieving voice.

"It's been taken care of," said Aya tossing the branch and the snake into the stream.

"Was it a viper?" I asked. I was already scared.

"If it were, I would have caught it alive. That was a rat snake. The liver of a live viper is made into medicine."

"Are there vipers in this mountain?"

"Yes."

That troubled me so I drank some beer.

Aya finished eating before everyone else and dragged over a large log and dumped it into the mountain stream. He gained a foothold on it and flew to the other shore. He clambered up the mountain cliff on the other side to pick wild edible plants like ginseng and thistle.

"That's dangerous. He shouldn't go to a dangerous place like that on purpose. Those plants grow in many other places," I said nervously, critical of Aya's adventure, "Aya is excited and definitely has the ulterior motive of showing off his bravery by putting himself in danger."

"That's true," said my niece agreeing with a wide smile.

"Aya!" I shouted, "Enough. It's dangerous. Enough already."

"Okay," he said and scrambled down the cliff. I was relieved.

On the way home, Yoko carried the plants gathered by Aya. For a long time, this niece has never been phased by much. On the way home, the "still ageless, healthy walker" tired in Sotogahama and went quiet. We descended the mountain to the song of cuckoos. Great loads of timber were piled up at the lumber mill on the outskirts of town. Trucks went back and forth endlessly. This is the scenery of a bountiful village.

"Kanagi shows spirit," I said to no one in particular.

"It does?" asked the son-in-law, who looked a little tired and sounded weary. Caught off balance I said, "No, well, I don't know much, but the Kanagi of ten years ago didn't feel like this. I remember a village in decline, not like it is now. The village felt like it was making a comeback."

At home, I told my oldest brother, the scenery of Kanagi was wonderful and had given me a renewed outlook. He said, "As you get older, you may come to find the landscape of the place where you were born and raised is better than Kyoto and Nara."

The next day, my oldest brother and his wife joined the previous day's party on an outing to Kanoko River Pond about six miles southeast of Kanagi. When we were about to leave, guests appeared at my brother's home, so we left without him. We went out dressed in monpe work pants and wearing white tabi socks and zori sandals. After walking a long way, close to five miles, this may have been the first time my sister-in-law has been to Kanagi since marrying. The weather was fair that day, too, but hotter. Guided by Aya, we plodded along the logging railway track by the Kanagi River. The distance between railroad ties on the track was narrower than one step but wider than half a step. This was exasperating and made walking complicated. I tired, soon stopped talking, and only wiped off sweat. When the weather is too good, the traveler becomes exhausted and discouraged.

"This area is a remnant of a great flood," Aya stopped

to explain. Huge stumps and logs scattered over several hectares of fields near the river reminded me of traces of a battlefield. The previous year, Kanagi was hit by a huge flood unlike anything the eighty-eight-year-old grandmother in our family had ever seen.

"All the trees flowed here from the mountains," said a mournful Aya.

"This is terrible," I said while wiping off my sweat, "It looks like the ocean came."

"Yes, like the ocean."

We left the Kanagi River and climbed for a while along the Kanoko River and finally left the track of the logging railway. Where we turned a little to the right, there was a large pond more than a mile around. A lone bird chirped. The surface of the blue water filling the lake was still. The area was a deep ravine called Souemon-sawa. Kanoko River at the bottom of the ravine recently dammed creating this large pond in Showa year 16 (1941).

A large stone monument near the pond was inscribed with the name of my oldest brother. The red earth of the cliff left by construction around the pond was still freshly exposed. The so-called natural glory was missing. But the strength of the village called Kanagi could be felt. This sort of personal success must produce a pleasant landscape. The careless travel critic stops to smoke a cigarette and organize his haphazard impressions while looking all around. The confident me led the group on a walk around the pond.

"This is nice. This area is nice," I said and sat in the shade of a tree on the promontory of the lake, "Aya, please tell me, is this a sumac tree?"

I would continue with this trip even if I broke out in a rash although racked with melancholy. He said it wasn't a sumac tree.

"Uh, that tree...what is it? It looks suspicious. Please find out," I said. Everyone laughed but I was serious. He said that wasn't sumac either. Thoroughly relieved, I decided to open my bento box there. I drank beer and conversed cheerfully. I excitedly talked about the time in second or third grade when I went on a school trip to a placed called Takayama on the west coast about seven miles from Kanagi and saw the sea for the first time.

The teacher who led the excursion had been excited for some time, lined us up in two lines facing the sea, and made us sing the song *Ware wa Umi no Ko* (I am a Child of the Sea).

> I am a child of the sea
> In the pine grove on the beach
> The whitecapped waves play

However, because this was our first glimpse of the sea in our lives, our singing of this song of children born on the shore was stilted. My child's heart felt embarrassed and uncomfortable.

I was zealous about my eccentric clothes for that trip. As instructed, I wore a straw hat with a wide brim, carried a plain wood cane cleanly branded several times at the temple and used by my older brother to climb Mount Fuji, received a pair of the lightest possible straw sandals from the teacher, was the only student wearing useless hakama trousers, and wore high-laced shoes with long socks. I started out playing the toady. Before we walked two miles, I was exhausted and first took off my hakama and shoes. One of the sandals was made from red cord and the other was straw. I had been given mismatched, worn out, miserable sandals. Soon I took off my hat and had someone else carry my cane. Finally, I was riding in the cart hired by the school for the sick. When I got home, not a speck of the brilliance I had when I set out remained. My shoes were dangling from one hand and I clutched the cane. When told about my condition, everyone laughed.

"Hey," a voice called. It was my oldest brother.

"Hey," we all called back. Aya ran to meet him. My brother appeared carrying an ice axe. Unfortunately, I drank every beer we had and was in bad shape.

My brother ate immediately, then we all walked toward the far side of the pond. We heard a loud rustling sound and a water bird took flight. The son-in-law and I looked at each other and for no reason nodded. Was it a goose or a duck? We asked with no confidence. At any rate, it was definitely wild waterfowl. We were struck by the energy of a ravine deep in a mountain. My brother walked in silence with his shoulders hunched. How many years had it been since I walked with my brother outside?

About ten years ago, my brother walked silently several steps ahead of me with his back hunched through a path in a field on the outskirts of Tokyo. I walked alone watching my brother from behind and sobbing; this may be the first time since then. I don't think he's forgiven me yet for that incident. It may be the worst event of my whole life. Nothing can be done about a cracked rice bowl. We can't go back. The people of Tsugaru, in particular, are a race that cannot forget a crack in the heart. After this, I thought I would not have another chance to walk outside with my brother again. I heard the sounds of water gradually getting louder.

At the edge of the pond was a famous local site called Kanoko Falls. Soon, the narrow falls just fifty feet high could be seen at our feet. We walked down a narrow path about a foot wide along the edge of Souemon-sawa. Immediately to our right, a mountain stood like a folding screen. To the left at our feet was a cliff. The basin of the waterfall at the bottom of the ravine coiled on itself producing a blue that made the basin look deeper.

"Oh, I'm feeling a bit dizzy," said my brother's wife half joking and walked timidly clinging to Yoko's hand.

Azaleas were in bloom on the mountainside to our right. My brother carrying the pickaxe on his shoulder went over to the azaleas blooming in their full glory and slackened his pace a little. Wisteria flowers were slowly beginning to open. The path gradually sloped downhill, and we followed it to the top of the waterfall. At the small mountain stream nearly six feet wide, tree stumps were placed near the center of the current. After gaining a foothold, it looks like the stream could be crossed in two quick steps. One by one, we jumped across. Only my sister-in-law was stranded.

"It's no good," she idly said and smiled but did not try to cross. She crouched and did not move one leg forward.

"Please carry her piggyback," my brother ordered Aya. Although Aya went to the other side, she only laughed and waved him away. This time, Aya displayed his superhuman strength. He came hugging a giant root and threw it at the top of the waterfall with a splash, and managed to build a bridge. My sister-in-law started to cross but her leg didn't move forward. She placed her hand on Aya's shoulder and finally crossed halfway. The rest of the way was shallow, and she jumped down into the river from the impromptu bridge and waded through the water. The hem of her monpe pants, her white tabi socks, and her sandals were soaking wet.

"I'm ready to return home from Takayama," said my sister-in-law and smiled like she recalled my pitiful appearance after returning home from my earlier excursion to

Takayama. Both Yoko and her husband burst out laughing, and my brother turned around.

"Huh? What?" he asked. Everyone stopped laughing. My brother looked odd, I thought he was waiting for an explanation. My story was too stupid, and I lacked the courage to begin the history of the "Return from Takayama." My brother said no more and walked off. My oldest brother was always alone.

5

THE WEST COAST

As I've explained many times before, although I was born and raised in Tsugaru, until today, I knew next to nothing about the land of Tsugaru. Aside from "Going to Takayama" in second or third grade on the west coast on the Sea of Japan side of Tsugaru, I never went anywhere. Takayama is nothing more than a fairly large village with a population close to five thousand people. Takayama is reached by leaving Kanagi and going due west by rickshaw about eight and a half miles. The shrine to Oinari-san on a small mountain on the coast is soon reached and is said to be a famous site. I remember some events from my youth, but only the failure of that outfit remains strong in my heart. All of what follows is rambling and hazy. From early on, I included plans to take this opportunity to tour the west coast of Tsugaru.

The day after going to the pond at Kanoko River, I left Kanagi for Goshogawara. Around eleven in the morning, I changed to the Gono Line at Goshogawara station and in less than ten minutes arrived at Kizukuri Station, which is on the Tsugaru Plain. I thought a short tour around this town was in order. When I got off, I saw a quiet, old town. The population was no more than four thousand, smaller than Kanagi's, but the town had an old history. I dully listened to the clanging sounds flowing from the machinery in a rice polishing mill. Somewhere under the eaves, a pigeon sang. My father was born in this place.

The generations of my family in Kanagi were only the women; the son-in-laws usually married into the family. My father was the third son in an old family called M in this village and became the whatever-generation head of the family having married into the family. Because my father died when I was fourteen, I can't say I knew my father as a *human*. I'll borrow a passage from my work *Memories*.

My father was a very busy man and rarely home. Even when home, he wasn't with the children. I feared my father. I wanted my father's fountain pen but never said so. I agonized alone over various matters. One night, I was talking in my sleep in bed with my eyes shut. I softly called, "Fountain pen. Fountain pen," to my father in conversation with a guest in the adjoining room. Naturally, it didn't seem to enter my father's ears or heart.

When my younger brother and I went inside the huge rice granary packed with bags of rice and played, my father stood in a wide stance at the entrance and shouted, "Get out of here. You brats." The huge shadow of my father with the light behind him looked black. Even now I think about my terror at that time and feel horrible... The following spring, while the snow was still piled high, my father coughed up blood and died in a hospital in Tokyo.

A local newspaper reported on my father's death in a special edition. Since his death, I was agitated by the sensation of it all. My name appeared in the newspaper mixed in with the names of the bereaved family. My father's corpse was laid in a large coffin, placed on a sleigh, and returned home. I went with many townspeople to a nearby village. I gazed at the hoods of some number of sleighs slipping out from the shadow of the forest under the moonlight and was transfixed. The next day, the people in my house gathered in the altar room where my father's coffin lay. When they removed the lid from the coffin, everyone's weeping voices rose. My father seemed to be sleeping. The high bridge of his nose was pale. Hearing everyone crying made my tears flow.

This may be about the only matter I can remember about my father. After he died, I felt the same admiration I had for my father toward my oldest brother. For that reason, I had peace of mind and relied on him and never once felt lonely for not having a father. However, as I got older, I disrespectfully speculated about my father's personality. My father also appeared in my dreams during my naps in the thatched hut in Tokyo. He actually had not died and was hiding for some political reason. He was a little older and more tired than the father I remember. While I longed for his presence, talking about dreams is inconsequential. At any rate, my interest in my father intensified recently.

All of my father's brothers had weak lungs. My father did not have tuberculosis but died after vomiting blood caused by some kind of obstruction in his respiratory tract. He died at fifty-three years old. With my child's mind, I believed someone was senile at that age and had a peaceful death. Now, I've come to consider death at fifty-three as being far from a peaceful death in one's declining years but a horrible death at a young age. If my father had lived a little longer, I had the conceit that he may have accomplished great work on behalf of Tsugaru. I wanted to see the house where my father was born and the town where he grew up.

The town of Kizukuri was only one road with houses standing on both sides. Fine paddy fields were cultivated behind the houses. Poplar trees stood scattered around the paddy fields. This is the first time I saw poplar trees on this trip to Tsugaru. Although I have seen them many times, no vivid memories remain of the poplars of Kizukuri. The light green, young leaves of the poplar swayed in a light breeze. Tsugaru Fuji seen from here is not very different than the view from Kanagi and has a fragile, graceful form. The legend goes that rice and beautiful women are produced in locations where this beautiful mountain profile can be seen. Rice is certainly abundant in this region. On the other hand, I wonder about the beautiful women. Like Kanagi, this place is also a little desolate. Concerning this point, I suspect that legend may be the reverse. In lands where the beauty of Mount Iwaki is visible, no, I will say no more. This sort of talk is liable to cause problems, so it may not be reasonable for a traveler passing through to make hasty conclusions.

The weather was excellent on that day, too. A misty smoke hovered like a fine spring haze over the straight concrete road leading from the railway station. I was affected by the spring heat and walked with my brain in a fog. I mispronounced the kanji characters on the bulletin board at the Kizukuri Police Station as the Mokuzou Police Station, a police station made of wood. Of course, I was convinced the building was made of wood *mokuzou* and anxiously gave a wry smile.

Kizukuri was a town of *komohi* sheltered sidewalks.

Long ago, komohi protected against the afternoon sun rays in Ginza. A tent to block the sun was stretched in front of every shop. The reader could walk under the tents to cool his face and think of it as a long, unplanned corridor. That long corridor was not constructed from tents but from the eaves of each house extended about six feet out and well built to last. There's no doubt the komohi are from the north country. They were not built to ward off the sun's rays. They aren't stylish. The eaves built close to each other make contacting neighbors easier when snow accumulates in the winter, and long corridors are created. And during blizzards, you can go out and shop with ease without fear of being exposed to the snowstorm. The most useful aspect is the absence of the danger found when children use Tokyo's sidewalks as a playground. On rainy days, this long corridor is a godsend to pedestrians. And for a traveler like me who's beaten by the spring heat will fly inside to cool off and be glared at by the annoyed people sitting in the shops. These corridors are appreciated. Although it is generally believed that komohi is the local word for *komise* (small shop), I think it fits the kanji for *konose* (hidden shallows) or *komohi* (hidden sun), but is not easily understood. I pondered this to amuse myself. While strolling down the komohi I came to M's Pharmaceutical Wholesale.

I didn't stop but passed by, as I walked straight down the komohi, I wondered what to do. This town's komohi is rather long. Although there are structures called komohi in the old towns of Tsugaru, few towns are like Kizukuri that depends on komohi that run through the entire town. Finally, I decided Kizukuri was the town of komohi. I walked a little while longer, and the komohi ran out at last. I did an about-face, sighed, and went back.

I never visited M's house before, not once, or Kizukuri.

Perhaps, someone brought me here to play when I was young, but I have no memories now. M, the head of the house, is an energetic man, four or five years older than me and a friend who visited Kanagi now and then for many years. Even if I visited him now, he would not look displeased, but my visit would be without warning. If I called on M for no particular reason as I groveled and smiled, he may out of surprise say something like, "This guy went broke in Tokyo and has come here to borrow money." One time before I die, I want to see the house where my father was born and felt terribly smug.

A man old enough to know better shouldn't talk like that. While walking, I agonized over whether I should go home. Again I found myself in front of M's Pharmaceutical Wholesale. I may not have a second chance. Being disgraced doesn't bother me. I'm going in. I immediately prepared to enter.

"Excuse me," I called into the shop.

M came out. "Ah, hey. Well, well," he stuttered with excitement and invited me to come into the sitting room without speaking and forced me to sit in front of the alcove.

"Hey, bring sake," he called to others in the house. In a few minutes, the sake arrived. In fact, it came quickly.

"It's been a long time. So long," said M as he gulped down his drink, "How long has it been since you've been in Kizukuri?"

"Let me see. I came when we were kids, so about thirty years."

"Yes, it's been that long. Well, please drink. You've come to Kizukuri, so make yourself at home. It's great you came. It's truly wonderful you're here."

The floor plan of the house was fairly close to that of our house in Kanagi. I heard that the current house in

Kanagi underwent major renovations using a design by my father when he arrived in Kanagi as the son-in-law who married into his bride's family and took their name, but the changes didn't matter. My father simply went to Kanagi and reproduced the identical floor plan of his birth home in Kizukuri. I thought about the mental state of my father as the son-in-law and smiled. This led me to ponder the similarities in the arrangement of plants and rocks in the garden. By discovering this minor fact, I felt like I touched the *human* of my late father. I thought this was the reason I came to M's house. M was determined to entertain me.

"No thank you, I've had enough. I have to catch the one o'clock train to Fukaura."

"To Fukaura? What will you do there?"

"Nothing special. I just want to see it one time."

"Are you writing?"

"Yes, I'm doing that too."

I couldn't say something to him that would spoil the fun like "I don't know when I'm going to die."

"So you'll write about Kizukuri. If you're writing about Kizukuri…," said M candidly, "First of all, you should write about the quantity of rice delivered. By comparing the jurisdictions of the police stations, the jurisdiction of the Kizukuri Police Station is first in the nation. Why? It is Japan's best. I believe it does no harm to say it is a monument to our hard work. When the water dried up in a band of fields in this area, I went to the neighboring villages for water and was very successful. I transformed into a huge tiger and was called the Water Tiger God. We're also landowners and have no time to fool around. Despite my bad back, I weed the fields. This time, I'll supply you and your people in Tokyo with a lot of good rice."

He was utterly dependable. Since we were small, M had a generous spirit. His big, round eyes, like a child's, were filled with charm. All the people in this area seemed to love and respect him. I prayed in my heart for M's happiness. Being delayed made me break into a sweat, but I left and was able to make the one o'clock train to Fukaura.

About thirty minutes after leaving Kizukuri on the Gono Line, the train passed Narusawa and Ajigasawa. Tsugaru Plain comes to an end in this area. Then the train ran along the coast of the Sea of Japan. I gazed through the window on my right at the sea and was soon admiring the mountains at the northern end of the Dewa hills as they evolved in about an hour into the scenic beauty of Odose. The rocks in this area are all sharp, jagged rocks of volcanic ash. This bedrock had been eroded flat by the sea and spotted with green. It erupted from the sea like a monster at the end of the Edo period and became a parlor large enough to hold a banquet for hundreds of people on the beach. This place was dubbed *Senjojiki* (a thousand tatami mats). Places here and there in this bedrock had sunken into curved shapes. When flooded with seawater, they resembled large cups filled to the brim with sake. This place should be called the Swamp of Cups, but the many large holes with diameters from one to two feet resembling cups led to the name of the Big Boozer.

If bizarre rock formations were chiseled on the seashore in this area and those tentacles continuously washed by angry waves, it's probably written about in guidebooks about famous places. Lacking an air of eeriness like the seashore in the northern end of Sotogahama, it becomes an ordinary *landscape* to the rest of the country. The atmosphere is not particularly hard to understand by people from other provinces who say it's the rigidity peculiar to Tsugaru. In short, Tsugaru is opening up to the world but is underrated in the eyes of people accustomed to it. In *A Brief History of Aomori Prefecture*, Takeuchi Umpei wrote that a long time ago, the region south of this area was not a part of Tsugaru but of Akita. In year 8 of Keicho (1603), after consulting with the neighboring Satake clan, this land was incorporated into the Tsugaru domain. This is only the irresponsible intuition of a vagabond like me, but somehow this area does not feel like Tsugaru. The unfortunate fate of Tsugaru is missing. The *essential badness* particular to Tsugaru is not in this area. I knew only by looking at the mountain streams. All of them were wise, culturally speaking. A stupid arrogance is missing.

About forty minutes after leaving Odose, the train arrived in Fukaura. This port town looked like the fishing villages near the shore in Chiba. With unassuming and gentle expressions on their faces, in less flattering terms, not too bright and cunning expressions, they welcome visitors with silence. After all, they exhibit total indifference to travelers. I would never say this atmosphere in Fukaura is a shortcoming. Without those expressions, I think living in this world is sometimes too much for people. Their expressions may be those of mature adults. Their confidence is submerged deep inside.

There is none of the childish, futile resistance seen in the northern part of Tsugaru. North Tsugaru seems half-cooked and not fully cooked like this place. Ah, that's it. I understand when I compare the two. The truth is people living in the interior of Tsugaru do not have confidence in their history. It's all gone. Thus, they recklessly stand up to a constant stream of insults from others like "This is going to be vulgar" and must assume an insolent attitude. That evolves into the rebellious, stubborn, and unyielding nature of the Tsugaru native and may shape his sorrowful, lonely fate. People of Tsugaru, raise your heads! Were you the people unafraid to affirm the pent-up force emerging just before the Renaissance in this land? When the glory of Japanese civilization shrinks and comes to an end, will the largely unfinished land of Tsugaru somehow become the hope of Japan? Those were my thoughts one night but I soon awkwardly stretched my shoulders. Confidence instigated by others is pointless. I don't know, but shouldn't one act, believe, and persevere for a time?

Today, the population of Fukaura is about five thousand and is the port on the southern edge of the west coast of old Tsugaru. During the Edo period, Fukaura was placed under the magistrate of the four bays with Aomori, Ajigasawa, and Jusan, and was one of the most important ports of the Tsugaru clan. The tranquil, small bay with deep waters formed between the hills is a scenic spot on the coast equal to the strange rock formations of Azuma Beach, Benten-jima Island, and Yukiai-zaki.

The town was quiet. Large, nice-looking diving suits hung upside down in the gardens to dry. I felt a deep calm with some element of despair. I walked straight down the road to the Deva gate of the Engaku-ji Temple just outside of town. The Physician of Souls shrine is designated a national treasure. I entered and thought about going home from Fukaura.

This perfect town left the traveler feeling lonely again. I went down to the beach, sat on a rock, and puzzled over what to do now. The sun was still high in the sky. Out of the blue, thoughts of my child in our *thatched hut* in Tokyo came to mind. I would have preferred not having those thoughts but my child's face targeted a void in my heart and leaped into my breast. I stood and headed to the post office. I bought a postcard and wrote a short update to the home I left in Tokyo. The child had whooping cough. And her mother would soon give birth to a second child.

Unable to bear my feelings, I randomly entered an inn, was led to a dirty room, and while removing my gaiters, I asked for sake. Faster than I expected, a tray and sake arrived. The promptness brought me a bit of relief. Although the room was dirty, the tray was piled with sea bream and abalone prepared in various ways. The sea bream and abalone appeared to be specialty products of this port. I drank two bottles of sake, but it was still too early to sleep.

Since coming to Tsugaru, others have treated me to meals. I had the trifling thought, Today is the one time I've drunk a lot of sake through my own efforts. I caught the young twelve- or thirteen-year-old girl who brought me the tray and asked if there was any more sake. She said, "No." Then I asked if there was another place to drink, she promptly said, "Yes." I was relieved and asked for directions to this drinking establishment. I went. It was a surprisingly tidy, little restaurant. I was escorted to a ten-tatami room overlooking the sea on the second floor. I sat cross-legged at the *Tsugaru-nuri* lacquered tray and said, "Sake. Sake." Only sake immediately appeared. I was grateful. The food took time, and the guest waited alone. A fortyish granny with missing front teeth quickly appeared carrying only a sake bottle. I thought I would ask her to tell me a Fukaura legend.

"What are the famous spots in Fukaura?"

"Did you visit Kannon-san?"

"Kannon-san? Oh, if by Kannon-san you mean the Engaku-ji Temple then yes."

I believed I could listen to some ancient story from this granny. However, a fat young woman appeared in this parlor and curiously made a joke. Given no choice, I thought, as a man, I should be direct.

I asked, "Would you please go downstairs?"

I'm giving advice to the reader. A man goes to a restaurant and must be forthright when speaking. I've had bitter experiences. When this young woman swelled up and stood, the old woman also stood and they left together. One being expelled from the room and the other sitting quietly wouldn't be unjust even from the perspective of love and justice between friends. I drank the sake alone in the huge room and gazed at the fire of the lighthouse in Port Fukaura. My melancholy only deepened and I returned to the inn.

The following morning, while I wondered if I would eat breakfast feeling lonesome, the proprietor came carrying a tray and a small dish.

"Are you Tsushima-san?" he asked.

"Yes," I said. I had written my pen name Dazai in the register.

"All right. I thought you looked familiar. I was a classmate in middle school of your brother Eiji. I didn't know the name Dazai you wrote in the register, but you looked very familiar."

"Oh, it's an alias."

"Yes, yes, I know. I heard about a younger brother who changed his name and wrote novels. I'm sorry about last night. Please have some sake. This is a small dish of salted abalone intestines, a good side dish for sake."

I finished my meal and enjoyed one salted intestine, which was good. In fact, it was delicious. I came to the edge of Tsugaru, and of course, I am grateful for the reach of the powers of my older brothers. In the end, I realized I can't do one thing through my own efforts which made the intestines more of a delicacy. In short, what I found at this port was the sphere of influence of my older brothers. I boarded the train with my mind in a fog.

On the way home from Fukaura, I stopped at the old

port town of Ajigasawa. Near this town was the center of the west coast of Tsugaru. During the Edo period, the port prospered as the dispatch point of much of Tsugaru's rice and the depot of Japanese-style boats to and from Osaka. Marine products were abundant. The fish caught off this shore first landed near the castle and then crowded the dining tables of homes in each region of the vast Tsugaru Plain. But with the current population of four thousand, five hundred, fewer than in Kizukuri and Fukaura, the town is beginning to lose its former power to thrive.

Sometime long ago, I believe many mackerel were caught in Ajigasawa. However, when we were young, we rarely heard stories of the mackerel here, but it was famous for sandfish. Because sandfish are supplied to Tokyo these days, the reader may know about them. They're about six or seven inches long when scaled. They may be mistaken for sweetfish but seem too big. Among the specialty production on the west coast, Akita is the center of production.

Tokyoites said it was bad to season them with oil, but oil added a lightly seasoned flavor to us. In Tsugaru, we eat fresh sandfish from one side after cooking it in light soy sauce. It's not amazing for one person to eat up twenty or thirty with ease. I've often heard about sandfish clubs where the biggest eater gets a prize. The sandfish sent to Tokyo are stale and considered disgusting probably because the people have no idea how to cook them.

Sandfish is mentioned in glossaries for haiku poets. I remember once reading the verse of a poet from the Edo era in which *sandfish* meant the light flavor of sandfish or may be a delicacy to the worldly man of Edo. In either case, eating sandfish is nothing more than the enjoyment of the hearth in a Tsugaru winter. Sandfish are the reason I've known the name of Ajigasawa since childhood. This was my first time seeing this town. A mountain is carried on the back of this town, which is slender and elongated. The streets of this town were smelly and had strangely stale, sweet and sour smells reminiscent of the verses of Boncho. The river waters were also murky. I was a bit tired. This town had long komohi like Kizukuri but was a little decrepit. The cold isn't as bad as in Kizukuri. The weather was excellent that day. Even if I walked down the komohi to avoid the sun, I had a queer sensation of choking. There seemed to be many restaurants. Long ago, there were so-called high-quality sake shops, but they have long since disappeared from developed areas. A total of four or five soba noodle shops remains. Nowadays, they call out to passersby with the unusual "Come in. Take a break."

At exactly noon, I entered a soba shop to rest. For forty *sen*, I enjoyed two servings of yakisoba. The broth was not bad. At any rate, this town was long. One street follows the coast, so no matter how far you go, the rows of houses don't change but continue on. I felt like I walked about two and a half miles when I finally reached the edge of town and turned around. This town had no center. The power of the town center in most towns hardens in one place that becomes the force of the town. Travelers simply passing through may feel they've reached the pinnacle at the center of town. Ajigasawa does not have one. It felt like the pivot of a fan had broken and it came apart. Going back and forth in my heart like a typical Degas-style political discussion wondering whether the rivalry for power among the towns causes problems, the pivot to this forlorn town is somewhere.

As I write this, I force a faint smile. If dear friends of mine had been in Fukaura and Ajigasawa to happily greet me, welcome my visit, and show me around, I would foolishly throw away my intuition and write with emotion-laden brush strokes about the stylishness of Tsugaru in Fukaura and Ajigasawa. In fact, the notes of a traveler are treacherous. If the people of Fukaura and Ajigasawa read this book, I hope they form a muted smile and give me a pass. Essentially, I have no intention of sullying their hometowns in my notes.

I left Ajigasawa on the Gono Line back to Goshogawara and arrived at two o'clock in the afternoon. I went straight from the station to Nakahata's home. I planned to write a lot about Nakahata in a series of works entitled *Kikyorai* (I Quit My Job and Moved Back Home) and *Kokyou* (Hometown). I didn't come here repeatedly, but he is my benefactor who settled the many untidy matters of my twenties without showing the least bit of disgust. Nakahata, who hasn't been himself for a long time, has a miserable, deep addiction. Last year, he fell ill and lost a great deal of weight.

"It's the times. You came here from Tokyo looking like that," he said sadly. He studied my figure that resembled a beggar and said, "And your socks are torn." He stood and took out a fine pair of socks from his chest and gave them to me.

"From here, I may want to go to a chic town."

"Yes, that would be nice. Go enjoy yourself. Keiko will show you the way," said Nakahata. Despite being terribly thin, his wit was as quick as ever. My aunt's family in Goshogawara lives in a fashionable town. When I was young, this town was called Hikara (Trendy Town) but now appears to go by another name, Omachi (Big Town). As I said in the introduction, I have many memories of my youth in Goshogawara. Four or five years ago, I published the following essay in a Goshogawara newspaper.

My aunt lives in Goshogawara and I've been visiting there since I was little. I went to the opening of the Asahi-za theater. I think I was in third or fourth grade. Sauemon definitely performed. His portrayal of Ume no Yoshibei made me cry. That was the first time I saw a revolving stage and was so surprised I jumped to my feet. Soon after that Asahi-za burned down in a fire. I clearly saw that fire from Kanagi. They say the fire broke out in the projection room. Ten grammar school students there to watch a movie were burned to death. The projectionist was charged with the crime of negligent homicide. In my child's heart, I could not forget the charge against the projectionist or his fate. I heard the rumor the theater burned down because the name Asahi-za contained the kanji character for *fire* in its name. This incident happened twenty years ago.

When I was seven or eight, I was walking through the bustling Goshogawara and fell in a ditch. It was pretty deep and the water reached my neck. It may have been three feet high. It was night. A man above me held out his hand and I grabbed it. I was pulled up and stripped naked in public. That was a problem. We were right in front of a secondhand clothes dealer. I was quickly dressed in old clothes from that store. It was a girl's *yukata* summer kimono. The obi was a *heko obi* sash. I was mortified. My aunt with her face drained of color came running. I grew up being spoiled by this aunt. I've never been good-looking. I was teased and became a little distrustful. This aunt was the only one who said I was a fine boy. When others made fun of my looks, she actually got mad. These are all memories from long ago.

Kei-chan, Nakahata's only daughter, and I left his house.

"I'd like to see the Iwaki River. Is it far?"

She said it was near.

"Well, let's go."

Guided by Kei-chan, I think we walked through the town for five minutes and came to a big river. I remember my aunt taking me a number of times to the riverbank but remember it being further away. With a child's legs, even this way probably feels very long. Also, I was afraid to go out and stayed inside, so when I went outside, I got tense and dizzy. It seemed so far away. There's the bridge. I definitely remember the long bridge I see now.

"I think that's called Inui Bridge."

"Yes, it is."

"What is the kanji character for *inui*? Is it the kanji for the direction northwest?"

"Yes, that's it," she said smiling.

"You don't look confident, are you? That's all right. Let's cross."

I leisurely crossed the bridge resting one hand on the handrail. The view was great. This river looked most like the canal of the Arakawa River in the suburbs of Tokyo. Haze rose from the grasses at the edge of the riverbanks and dazzled the eyes. The Iwaki River flowed a brilliant white while lapping the grasses at the edges of both shores.

"In the summer, everyone cools off here. There's nowhere else to go."

I thought the people of Goshogawara loved to have fun and that was probably lively.

"The new building over there is the Shokondo Shrine for the war dead," said Kei-chan and pointed upstream along the river. She quietly smiled and said, "Shokondo is the pride of my father."

The building looked magnificent. Nakahata was a leader of the war veterans. To rebuild this Shokondo, he no doubt ran around displaying his customary chivalry. We crossed the bridge and stood at its foot talking for a short time.

"The apple trees have been cut a little to thin them. I've heard that after the cutting, potatoes or something else is planted."

"Doesn't it differ depending on the soil? That's what they say around here."

There are apple fields in the shadows of the banks of the big river. Their white flowers were in full bloom. The sight of the flowers of the apple trees reminded me of the scent of face powder.

"I received many apples from Kei-chan, too. Next, you'll receive a groom."

"Yes," she calmly said and thoughtfully nodded.

"When? Will it be soon?"

"The day after tomorrow."

"Really?" I was surprised, but she was unmoved like it was someone else's affair, "We should go back. You're probably very busy."

"No, not at all," she said too calmly. I silently admired the only daughter getting married in order to continue the family line. There's something different about her, although she's a young nineteen- or twenty-year-old woman.

"Tomorrow, I'm off to Kodomari," I replied and crossed the long bridge again and added, "I think I'll go see Take."

"Take. The Take who appeared in the novel?"

"Yes. Her."

"You must be very happy."

"Well, seeing her will be nice."

This time, I came to Tsugaru intent on seeing a certain person. I think of that person as my mother. I cannot forget that person's face although it's been close to thirty years. My whole life may have been decided by this person. Below is a passage from *Memories*.

> I clearly remember turning six or seven. A nursemaid called Take read books to me. We read many books together. Take was obsessed with my education. I was sickly and read many books when confined to bed. If I ran out of books to read, she borrowed children's books from the Sunday school in the village and let me read them. I remember silently reading them. No matter how many I read, I never tired. Take also taught me morals. She often took me to the temple to show and explain *Oekakeji* about hell and paradise. Anyone who sets fires has to carry a blazing basket on his back. The body of a man with a mistress is wrapped by a green snake with two heads and is suffocated. When you reach places like a lake of blood, a mountain of pins, and *Avichi*, a deep hole with no known bottom enveloped by white smoke, pale, thin people barely open their mouths and scream. If you tell a lie, you go to hell and your tongue is cut out for a demon. When I heard these things, I got so scared I cried.
>
> Behind the temple was a small, elevated graveyard. Many stupa shrines were erected like a forest along the hedges of flowers like roses. A black iron ring like a wheel as big as the full moon was attached to each stupa. The ring clattered as it turned. Take told me if the ring comes to a standstill and does not move again, the person who turned it goes to paradise. If it stops and begins to turn in the opposite direction, the person goes to hell. When Take turned, a pleasant sound was raised as it turned for a short time and it always quietly stopped. However, by chance, when I turned it, the ring went in reverse. I remember

going to the temple alone one autumn and turning one of those metal rings. And one day it clattered and turned in reverse as everyone said. While suppressing a fit of rage about to erupt, I persisted in turning it dozens of times. Nightfall came and I left the graveyard in despair....

Eventually, I entered grammar school in my hometown. My memories of that time shift. Before I knew it, Take disappeared and went to be a wife in some fishing village. Was she worried I would follow her? Without a word to me, she suddenly disappeared. During the Obon Festival the next year, Take came to my house, but I gave her the cold shoulder. She asked about my grades, but I didn't answer. I would have told anyone else. Take said, "Overconfidence leads to failure," and did not praise me too much.

My mother was sick and I didn't drink one drop of my mother's milk and was cradled by a wet nurse immediately after birth. When I turned three and toddling around, my wet nurse left. In her place, a nursemaid named Take was hired. At night, I slept cuddled by my aunt, but the rest of the time, I was always with Take. From three to eight years old, I was raised by Take. Then one morning, I woke with a start and called to Take, but she didn't come. I was surprised and knew something had happened. I screamed and cried. I wailed with the heartbreaking thought, Take's gone! Take's gone! I sobbed convulsively for the next few days.

Even today, I cannot forget the pain of that time. One day a year later, I bumped into Take, but she acted strangely aloof, which enraged me. I never saw her again. Four or five years earlier, I was asked to be a guest on the radio broadcast *Furusato ni Yoseru Kotoba* (Words to My

Hometown). I read a passage about Take from *Memories*. When I think of home, I remember Take. She probably did not hear the broadcast of my reading.

There was no news and has not been any to this day. From the start of this trip to Tsugaru, my long-cherished wish was to see Take. I am interested in enjoying the self-control of saving the good thing for last. My going to the port in Kodomari was the last item of this trip's itinerary.

No, before going to Kodomari, I thought I would go to Hirosaki right after Goshogawara, walk the streets of Hirosaki, go to the Owani Hot Springs, spend one night there, and finally go to Kodomari. I was gradually disheartened by the small amount remaining of my travel expenses from Tokyo. Was I tired of traveling? From here on, I will be drained by walking around here and there. I gave up on going to the Owani Hot Springs and changed my plan of going to Hirosaki on my way back to Tokyo. I made up my mind to spend the night at my aunt's home in Goshogawara and tomorrow go straight to Kodomari. I went with Kei-chan to my aunt's home in Trendy Town, but my aunt was out. Her grandchild was ill and had been admitted to a hospital in Hirosaki, and she went to attend to the child.

My cousin smiled and said, "Mother knew you were coming and wanted to see you. She called and asked for you to go to Hirosaki."

My aunt arranged for this cousin to marry a doctor, who would take their family name.

"Oh, I'm thinking about going to Hirosaki on my way back to Tokyo and will be sure to stop by the hospital."

"Tomorrow, you're going to Kodomari to see Take," said Kei-chan, who despite being busy with her own preparations, did not return home but spent time with us.

"To see Take," said my cousin with a sober look, "That's nice. Who knows how happy Take would be."

My cousin seemed to understand how much I yearned to see Take."

I worried about how would we meet. Of course, there's no reason to make any arrangements. Simply relying on the knowledge of Koshino Take of Kodomari, I will pay a visit.

"I've heard there's only one bus a day to Kodomari," said Kei-chan and stood to examine the timetable hanging in the kitchen, "If you don't leave here on the first train tomorrow, you'll miss the bus leaving Nakazato. You can't get up late on that important day."

She seemed to have forgotten all about her own important day. The first train leaves Goshogawara at eight o'clock, travels north on the Tsugaru Railway, passes through Kanagi without stopping, and arrives at nine in Nakazato, the end of the line of the Tsugaru Railway. Then I will ride the bus to Kodomari for around two hours and arrive in Kodomari by noon tomorrow. At dusk, Kei-chan and I finally went home and met the Doctor (we've been calling the doctor groom by the proper noun for a long time) returning home from the hospital. We drank sake and I talked nonsense until midnight.

The next morning I was awakened by my cousin, gulped down breakfast, and rushed to the depot in time to catch the first train. Again, the weather was good. My head was in a fog and I had a hangover. Since there was no one scary at the house in Trendy Town, I drank a little too much the previous night. A cold sweat moistened my forehead. The refreshing morning sun shined into the train. Only I had the unbearable feeling of being muddy, dirty, and rotting. I always have this feeling of self-hatred after drinking too much sake. Perhaps, I've repeated this experience several thousand times but still lack the resolve to quit drinking. Because I'm a hard drinker, I tend to be taken lightly by others. If this world had no sake, I seriously believed the nonsense that I may have become a saint. While thinking these thoughts, I lazily stared out the window at the Tsugaru Plain. Finally, we passed Kanagi and arrived at Ashinokoen, a small station no bigger than a crossing guard station.

I recall an anecdote about the mayor of Kanagi. He tried to buy a ticket to Ashinokoen at Ueno Station in Tokyo and was told indignantly that no such station existed and no one had ever heard of Ashinokoen on the Tsugaru Railway. He made the station employee search for thirty minutes and finally obtained a ticket to Ashinokoen.

When I leaned out of the window and saw that tiny station, a young woman wearing a kimono of Kurume-kasuri cloth and monpe pants made from the same fabric was carrying a large bundle in a wrapping cloth under each arm. She ran to the ticket gate and, with her eyes slightly closed, gently offered her ticket in her mouth to the good-looking, young station attendant. The young man understood and moved his hand like a skilled dentist extracting a front tooth to the red ticket held between rows of bright white teeth and deftly clipped it with his scissors. Neither the young woman nor the young man smiled the tiniest smile. Their composure seemed ordinary. The young woman hopped on the train about to leave. It seemed like the engineer had been waiting for that young woman to board. This idyllic station resembles no other in the entire country. The mayor of Kanagi should shout "Ashinokoen!" in his loudest voice the next time he's at Ueno Station.

The train ran through a forest of larch trees. This area became Kanagi Park. I could see a marsh. Long ago, my older brother donated a sightseeing boat to this marsh. In no time we arrived in Nakazato, a small village with a population of four thousand. From this area on, Tsugaru Plain becomes narrow and small. When we arrived at the hamlets of Uchigata, Aiuchi, and Wakimoto north of here, the paddy fields were considerably smaller. This place could be called the North Gate of the Tsugaru Plain. When a boy, I came to visit a relative, a dry goods dealer named Kanamaru. I may have been four and only remember a waterfall at the edge of the village.

"Shuuuchiiiyaa," I was being called and turned to see Kanamaru's daughter standing there smiling. She must have been one or two years older than me but didn't look older.

"It's been a long time. Where are you going?"

"To Kodomari," I said, impatient to see Take. I paid attention to nothing else.

"Well, my bus is here. Excuse me, bye."

"On your way back, please stop by the house. We built a new house on top of that mountain."

When I looked in the direction she was pointing, a new house stood alone on top of a small mountain of greenery to the right of the station. Even though she wasn't Take, I was happy to have this chance encounter with a familiar face from my childhood and will stop by that new house to ask about Nakazato. For no reason, I was impatient with no time to lose.

"Well, be seeing you," we separated exchanging pleasantries and I hopped on the bus.

The bus was crowded. I had to stand for the two-hour trip to Kodomari. This would be the first time in my life I would see Nakazato and parts further north. The Ando clan called the forefathers of the Tsugaru lived in this area. I discussed the prosperous Port Jusan earlier, but the center of the history of the Tsugaru Plain seems to lie between Nakazato and Kodomari. The bus traveled north along mountain roads. The roads looked bad and the bus shuddered. I clutched the horizontal bar of the luggage rack, rounded my back, and watched the scenery pass by the bus window.

So this is northern Tsugaru. Compared to the landscape of Fukaura, this place was wild everywhere. There was no scent of human skin. Mountain trees, thorny shrubs, and bamboo grass live with no relationship to humanity. Compared to Tappi on the eastern shore, this area was tamer. The grasses and trees were on the brink of being landscape. I didn't chat with any of the travelers. Lake Jusan turned a chilly white before my eyes.

The lake had an elegant but impermanent feeling like water filling a shallow pearl oyster. There was not one wave. Not one boat was floating on it. The quiet still lake was vast. It was a stagnant pool tossed out by people. The floating clouds and the shadows of flying birds felt like they couldn't be reflected on the surface of the lake. Soon after passing Lake Jusan, we appeared on the coast on the Sea of Japan. Because this area is crucial to national defense, as is the custom, I will avoid detailed descriptions.

A little before noon, I arrived at Port Kodomari. This port was the furthest north on the west coast of Honshu. Just over the mountain this far north is Tappi on the eastern shore. The hamlets on the west coast end here. In other words, this place was the reason I unexpectedly returned from Port Fukaura on the western shore of the old Tsugaru domain and came without resting to Port Kodomari on the northern end of the same shore centered on the Goshogawara area. This modest fishing village had a population of about two thousand, five hundred. From the Heian era, ships from other provinces entered and left this port. The boats passing through Ezo, in particular, always entered and anchored at this port to avoid strong easterly winds.

During the Edo period, mounds of rice and lumber were often shipped out from the nearby Port Jusan. I intended to write about that many times. Even now, the only port constructed in this village is splendid and does not fit the village. The paddy fields on the outskirts of the village are few, but the marine products are abundant. In addition to fish like pike, greenling, squid, and sardine, there are many marine plants like varieties of kelp and seaweed.

I got off the bus and began to approach people walking in the area to ask, "Do you know a woman named Koshino Take?"

"Koshino Take?" replied a middle-aged man wearing a government-mandated national uniform who may have been an official at the village hall. He looked puzzled and said, "A lot of families in this village have that last name Koshino."

"She used to live in Kanagi and should be around fifty years old," I eagerly said.

"Ah, I know her."

"Is she here? Where is she? Where is her house?"

Following his directions, I found Take's home. It was a small hardware store with an eighteen-feet-wide front. It was ten times more fabulous than my hut in Tokyo. The curtain was down at the shop front. It can't be, I thought. I ran up to the glass door at the entrance and, as expected, a small padlock was locked. I tried to open another glass door, but it didn't budge. She was out. At a loss, I wiped off the sweat. There is no possibility she has moved away.

Could she have gone out for a short time? But where? No, this is not Tokyo. When you step out for a little while in the country, you don't drop the curtain and close the doors. Maybe she'll be away for two or three days or longer. This is bad. Take went to some other village. It's possible. I was stupid to believe that knowing where she lived was enough. I tapped on the glass door and called, "Koshino-san! Koshino-san!" I didn't expect a reply. I sighed and walked diagonally across the street and into a tobacco shop. I said it seemed like nobody was at home at the Koshino's and asked the proprietress if she had any idea where Koshino-san had gone. The gaunt old woman nonchalantly said she was probably at the sports field day. I braced myself.

"So where is the field day being held? Is it nearby?"

She said it was close and to go straight down the road, past the paddy fields to the school. The field day is being held behind the school.

"She went out carrying a picnic box with the children this morning."

"Is that so? Thank you."

I followed her directions and came upon the paddy fields. I took the path between the paddy fields to the sand dunes. A national elementary school stood above the dunes. I went around to the back of the school to see and was stunned. I felt like I was dreaming. In this fishing village at the northern edge of Honshu, before my eyes appeared a lively festival so beautiful and little changed from long ago I was almost brought to tears. First, the flags of all nations flew high. Young women were gaily dressed. Daytime drunks were scattered here and there.

Around the perimeter of the athletic field, almost one hundred temporary huts were erected close together. No, there looked to be no empty places left around the field. The huts crowded together stood on straw mats on the small and large hills overlooking the field. They seemed to be taking a noon break. In the rooms of the one hundred small houses, a family spread out its picnic boxes. While the men drank sake, the women and children ate and talked and laughed under the clear skies. I couldn't stop thinking, Japan is a blessed country. It is surely the Land of the Rising Sun.

Even with the fate of the nation at stake in a major war, a lonely village on the northern edge of Honshu mysteriously holds this huge, merry banquet. The ancient gods observe the courageous smiles and the generous dances in this remote part of Honshu. I felt like I had become the hero in a fairy tale. In this fairy tale, I searched over seas and over mountains for my mother. I walked seven thousand miles and ended up in this province where splendid music and dance were being performed on these sandy dunes. I was compelled to search for the caretaker who raised me somewhere among the cheerful crowd playing music and dancing.

It's been close to thirty years since we parted. She had big eyes and red cheeks. She had a small red mole on her right or left eyelid. That's all I remembered. If I saw her, I would know. I was confident. Searching this crowd would be difficult, I thought while scanning the grounds and was on the verge of tears. I had no other options. I could only slowly walk around the field.

I gathered my courage to ask a lone youth, "Do you know where Koshino Take is? Do you know her? She's around fifty years old. She's Koshino from the hardware store." That was all I knew about Take.

"Koshino of the hardware store," said the youth as he thought, "Oh, I think she's in a hut over there."

"Okay, over there?"

"Yeah, I'm not really sure. I think you'll find her somehow. Go look."

The search was a major undertaking. I couldn't seem smug to the youth by telling him things like it's been thirty, long years. I thanked the young man and a little befuddled walked in the general direction he pointed but didn't know what to do. Finally, I poked my head into the huts of happy circles eating their lunches.

"Pardon me. I'm sorry to bother you, but is Koshino Take, uh, Koshino-san of the hardware store, here?"

"No," was the sharp reply from a frowning woman in a bad mood.

"Oh? Thank you. Excuse me. Have you seen her around here?"

"Uh, I don't know. Why? Are you the bonder man?"

I peeked into another hut to ask. They didn't know. Then another. I looked obsessed as I walked around asking, "Is Take here? Is Take from the hardware store here?" I made two rounds of the field but found nothing. I had a hangover. My throat was so parched I couldn't stand it. I went over to the school's well to have a drink of water and then returned to the athletic field. I sat on the sand, removed my jacket, and wiped away the sweat. With tired eyes, I watched the happy crowd of men and women, young and old.

She's here. She is definitely here. Unaware of my suffering, she's probably opening the picnic box and making the children eat. I imagined a school teacher shouting through a megaphone, "Koshino Take-san, you have a visitor," but that brutal method would be appalling. It would be inexcusable of me to create my joy by playing that over-the-top prank. It was not to be. The gods say when to meet. I'm going home. I put on my jacket and stood. Again I walked the footpath between the paddy fields back to the village.

Would the sports field day end around four o'clock?

That would be four more hours. Should I go lie down at a local inn and wait for Take to return home? While waiting disheartened in a dirty room in the inn, would I get mad wondering if Take was worth the wait? Given these feelings, I wanted to see Take, but it didn't seem I would. In other words, it was not in the stars. If I traveled all this way and know she's right there, returning home without seeing her may fit my essentially bad life so far. My plans spawned from ecstasy always ended up in chaos just like this. That is my awful fate. I'm going home.

Thinking about it, although she could be said to be the guardian who raised me, frankly, she was an employee. Isn't she a servant? Are you the servant's child? You're a man old enough to know better, but you adore the servant from long ago and want to see her. You're no good. My older brothers have the reasonable belief that I'm a vulgar, gutless sort. Among my brothers, I'm the sole oddball. Why am I so sloven, shabby, and a low life? You need to buck up.

I went to the bus depot and asked for the departure time of the bus. The last bus to Nakazato would leave at one-thirty. I decided to go home on that 1:30 bus. I had thirty more minutes here and was a little hungry. I entered a gloomy inn close to the depot and said, "I'm in a rush and would like to have lunch."

Regret remained in my heart. If this inn were pleasant, I would rest here until around four o'clock, but rejected the idea. A sickly-looking proprietress happened to peek out from inside to coldly inform me that everyone had gone to the sports field day, and there's nothing she could do.

I was resolved to go home and sat on a bench at the bus depot. After resting for about ten minutes, I stood and loitered around the area. All right, I'll try one more time. I'll go up to the front of Take's empty house. I will force a smile and bid farewell for life without anyone knowing. I went to the front of the hardware store and glimpsed an unlocked lock at the entrance. The door was ajar two or three inches. It was a gift from god! My courage multiplied one hundred times. I braced myself and pushed open a clattering glass door, which couldn't be described as shoddy but was inadequate.

"Excuse me. Excuse me."

The reply of "Yes" from inside was followed by the appearance of a fourteen- or fifteen-year-old girl in a sailor suit. Her face brought back Take's face. Forgetting my manners, I walked up to her in the room with the dirt floor and introduced myself.

"I'm Tsushima from Kanagi."

She took a sharp breath and laughed. Sometime in the past, Take may have told her children about raising a child named Tsushima. For that reason, the girl and I did not behave like strangers. I was grateful. I am Take's child. The servant's child, whatever, it didn't matter. I could shout, I am Take's child. My brothers can sneer at me, I don't care. I am this girl's brother.

"Oh, good," I said without thinking, "Take? Is she still at the field day?"

"Yes," she said not showing a bit of shyness and nodded, "My stomach hurts so I came home for medicine."

It's terrible to say, but that pain was a blessing. I thanked the belly ache and relieved I ran into this girl. It's all right now, I will see Take. I will cling to and not leave this child.

"I searched the field for a long time but didn't find her."

"Yes," she said and nodded a bit and pressed on her stomach.

"Does it still hurt?"

"A little."

"Did you take the medicine?"

She nodded.

"Does it hurt a lot?"

She smiled and shook her head.

"Well, I have a favor to ask. Could you take me to Take? Your stomach probably still hurts, but I've come a long way. Can you walk?"

"Yes," she gave a long nod.

"Excellent. I thank you."

She nodded twice, stepped down to the dirt floor, put on her geta clogs, pressed on her stomach, and left the house slightly bent over.

"Did you run in the field day?"

"Yes."

"Did you win a prize?"

"No."

She walked ahead of me and never stopped pressing her stomach. We passed through the path in the paddy fields, emerged from the sand dunes, and walked around to the back of the school. We cut across the center of the field then the girl trotted into a hut and soon Take came out. She looked blankly at me.

"I'm Shuji," I said smiling and took off my hat.

"Oh" is all she said. She didn't smile but looked serious. Just as quickly, her hard stance crumbled. Her nonchalant, weak tone sounded strangely resigned.

"Well, come in and watch the meet," she said and led me inside her hut.

"Please sit here," she said to have me sit beside her. Take said nothing but sat properly placing her hands on the round knees of her monpe pants and ardently watched the children running. However, I wasn't the least bit dissatisfied and completely at peace. I stretched out my legs and lazily watched the games. Not one thought was in my heart. I was free from worry and untroubled. What should I do? Is this how peace feels?

If so, I can say for the first time in my life I've experienced peace in my heart. My birth mother, who died a few years ago, was a fine mother. She was dignified and gentle. However, she never gave me this mysterious sense of relief. Shouldn't the mothers of the world give this sweet, abstract relief to their children? In that case, loyalty to one's parents is certain no matter what. While I greatly appreciate my mother, I didn't understand her falling ill and her inactivity. Loyalty to one's parents is a natural feeling and not ethics.

Take's cheeks were flush. A small red mole the size of a poppy seed was on her right eyelid. Her hair was specked with gray. Nevertheless, Take sitting properly beside me had changed little from the Take I remembered from my childhood. I later heard that Take entered service in my family and carried me on her back when I was three and she was fourteen. For the next six years, I was raised and taught by Take. The Take of my memories was definitely not a young girl but a mature woman not the least bit different from this Take now before my eyes.

And I later learned from Take, a deep blue belt with the iris pattern she was wearing that day was the same belt she wore while in service at my home. Around that time, my family gave her the light purple *haneri* neckpiece of her kimono. Perhaps, that's why I experienced a scent identical to my memories with Take sitting there. Maybe I'm biased, but all the other *Aba* (feminine form of *Aya*) in this fishing village seemed to have a high opinion of Take.

Her kimono was new handwoven cotton with stripes, and she wore monpe pants made of the same fabric. This striped pattern was not lively, but the selection was solid.

She was not trifling and had a strong bearing. I also kept quiet. After time passed, Take looked straight ahead at the field, rolled her shoulders, and released a long, deep sigh. That was the first time I understood Take was also serene but said nothing.

Take abruptly asked, "Have you eaten?"

"I'm fine," I said. I truly didn't want to eat.

"I have rice cakes," said Take and touched a picnic box arranged in a corner of the hut.

"I'm fine. I don't want to eat."

Take gave a little nod and asked no more.

"This one doesn't like rice cakes," she said softly with a smile. After close to thirty years of hearing no news about each other, she seemed to understand the hard drinker I became. It's a mystery. I grinned and Take frowned.

"You also smoke. You've smoked one after another for a while. I taught you to read books but not to smoke or drink," she said. That is an example of negligence inviting failure. I suppressed a smile.

I kept a straight face, but this time, Take smiled and stood.

"Shall we go see the cherry blossoms of the Dragon God?" she asked.

"Oh yes, let's go."

I followed Take up the sand dunes behind the hut. Violets bloomed on the dunes. Low wisteria vines spread out. Take climbed up without a word. I said nothing as I stumbled along. I climbed up slowly to the forest of the Dragon God. Double cherry blossoms opened here and there along the forest path. Take's hand reached out to break off a branch of double cherry blossoms. While walking, she plucked the flower from the branch and tossed in on the ground. She stopped, excitedly turned to me and words poured out like a dam broke.

"It's been a long time. At first, I didn't understand. My daughter said, 'Tsushima from Kanagi's here,' Impossible, I thought. I didn't believe you came to see me. Even when I came out of the hut and saw your face, I didn't understand. You said, 'I'm Shuji,' but I thought, Heavens! and could not speak. I saw nothing, not the sports field or anything else.

"For close to thirty years, I wanted to see you. I lived wondering if I'd ever see you again. You grew into a man and wanted to see me. Had you really come all the way to Kodomari to see me? Should I be thankful, happy, or sad? Which would be good? Well, it's good you came. When I went into service at your home, you were toddling around and falling, toddle and fall. You still didn't walk very well. When it was time to eat, you walked all around carrying your rice bowl. Your favorite place to eat was under the stone stairs in the storehouse.

"I told you old folk tales. While looking at my face, I fed you each bite. You were trouble, but I loved you. Now, you are this adult man, and all of that is like a dream. I went to Kanagi once in a while. Were you there when I was walking around Kanagi? I walked around and looked at every boy about your age. It's wonderful you came."

With each word spoken, like in a dream, she plucked a flower on the cherry blossom branch in her hand and threw it away.

"Do you have children?" she said and finally broke the branch and tossed it away. She squared her elbows and adjusted her monpe pants.

"How many?" she asked.

I approached a pine tree on the side of the path and answered, "One."

"Boy or girl?"

"A girl."

"How old is she?"

She fired off questions one after the other. I was moved by Take's expression of unrestrained love. I thought, Now that is Take. I realized that among my siblings, only I was childish and lacked composure. This was the effect of this unhappy foster parent. For the first time, I understood the essence of my upbringing. I concluded I am not a man with a polished upbringing. I don't come across as a child from a rich family.

The unforgettable people to me are T in Aomori, Nakahata in Goshogawara, Aya in Kanagi, and Take in Kodomari. Aya still serves my family today. The others were a part of my home one time long ago. I am their friend.

Although I'm not pretending these are the final writings of an old sage, this new record of the culture and geography of Tsugaru during a holy war resembles the confessions of a writer on a hunt for his friends. I think a serious mistake will not be committed by putting down my pen for a while. I still want to write, there's this and that. For the most part, I believe I've exhausted the stories about the vibrant atmosphere of Tsugaru. I was not ostentatious. I did not trick the reader. And reader, if alive, we'll meet another day. Go in health. Don't despair. Well, good-bye.

CREDITS

Japanese source text:

Dazai, Osamu. Tsugaru (津軽), Maedo Shuppansha, 1947. Retrieved from Aozora Bunko (https://www.aozora.gr.jp/cards/000035/card2282.html) (January 16, 2014).

Cover image:

Derived from: Asamushi Hot Springs Nebuta Festival - By 663highland [GFDL (http://www.gnu.org/copyleft/fdl.html), CC-BY-SA-3.0 (http://creativecommons.org/licenses/by-sa/3.0/) or CC BY 2.5 (https://creativecommons.org/licenses/by/2.5)], from Wikimedia Commons (https://commons.wikimedia.org/wiki/File:Asamushi_Onsen_Nebuta_Matsuri_Aomori_Japan05s3.jpg)

www.jpopbooks.com

ABOUT THE AUTHOR

Osamu Dazai (June 19, 1909 - June 13, 1948) was born Tsushima Shuji, the sixth son of a wealthy family in Aomori Prefecture. He was an important mid-twentieth century Japanese novelist and part of I-novel literary movement. His bestselling work was The Setting Sun (斜陽). His other works include *The Late Years* (晩年), *Schoolgirl* (女生徒), *Run, Melos!* (走れメロス), *New Hamlet* (新ハムレット), *Fairy Tales* (お伽草紙), *Villon's Wife* (ヴィヨンの妻), and *No Longer Human* (人間失格). He ended his life troubled by addictions and left unfinished the novel *Goodbye*.

Fron the Japanese Wikipedia page for Osamu Dazai (https://ja.wikipedia.org/wiki/%E5%A4%AA%E5%AE%B0%E6%B2%BB) (Retrieved July 17, 2018)

www.jpopbooks.com

Printed in the USA
CPSIA information can be obtained
at www.ICGtesting.com
CBHW021140301024
16655CB00007B/122